Cannery Row

John Steinbeck was born in Salinas, California, in 1902.
After studying science at Stanford University he worked
successively as labourer, druggist, caretaker, fruit-picker and
surveyor. His first novel, *Cup of Gold* (1929), was about
Morgan the pirate. *The Grapes of Wrath* (1939), his most
popular book, tells of a migratory family seeking work in
California; it was awarded the Pulitzer Prize, and has been
compared in its influence to *Uncle Tom's Cabin*. His other
novels include *East of Eden, Of Mice and Men, The Pearl,
Sweet Thursday* and *Cannery Row*, all published in Pan Books.
Also available in Pan are several collections of his short stories,
and *Journal of a Novel, The East of Eden Letters*. In 1962
Steinbeck was awarded the Nobel Prize for Literature.
He died in 1968.

Also by John Steinbeck
in Pan Books

The Pearl
Burning Bright
Sweet Thursday
The Short Reign of Pippin IV
The Log from the Sea of Cortez
East of Eden
The Winter of Our Discontent
The Moon is Down
Of Mice and Men
Tortilla Flat
The Long Valley
To a God Unknown
The Grapes of Wrath
The Acts of King Arthur and His Noble Knights

Once There Was A War
Travels with Charley
Journal of a Novel

John Steinbeck
Cannery Row

Pan Books in association with
William Heinemann

for Ed Ricketts
who knows why or should

First published in Great Britain 1945
by William Heinemann Ltd
This edition published 1974 by Pan Books Ltd,
Cavaye Place, London SW10 9PG
in association with William Heinemann Ltd,
19 18 17 16 15 14
All rights reserved
ISBN 0 330 24145 1
Printed and bound in Great Britain by
Hazell Watson & Viney Limited,
Member of the BPCC Group,
Aylesbury, Bucks

Cannery Row

CANNERY ROW

CANNERY ROW in Monterey in California is a poem, a stink, a grating noise, a quality of light, a tone, a habit, a nostalgia, a dream. Cannery Row is the gathered and scattered, tin and iron and rust and splintered wood, chipped pavement and weedy lots and junk heaps, sardine canneries of corrugated iron, honky-tonks, restaurants and whorehouses, and little crowded groceries, and laboratories and flop houses. Its inhabitants are, as the man once said, 'whores, pimps, gamblers, and sons of bitches,' by which he meant Everybody. Had the man looked through another peep-hole he might have said: 'Saints and angels and martyrs and holy men,' and he would have meant the same thing.

In the morning when the sardine fleet had made a catch, the purse-seiners waddle heavily into the bay blowing their whistles. The deep-laden boats pull in against the coast where the canneries dip their tails into the bay. The figure is advisedly chosen, for if the canneries dipped their mouths into the bay the canned sardines which emerge from the other end would be metaphorically, at least, even more horrifying. Then cannery whistles scream and all over the town men and women scramble into their clothes and come running down to the Row to go to work. Then shining cars bring the upper classes down: superintendents, accountants, owners who disappear into offices. Then from the town pour Wops and Chinamen and Polaks, men and women in trousers and rubber coats and oilcloth aprons. They come running to clean and cut and pack and cook and can the fish.

The whole street rumbles and groans and screams and rattles while the silver rivers of fish pour in out of the boats and the boats rise higher and higher in the water until they are empty. The canneries rumble and rattle and squeak until the last fish is cleaned and cut and cooked and canned and then the whistles scream again and the dripping, smelly, tired Wops and Chinamen and Polaks, men and women, straggle out and droop their ways up the hill into the town and Cannery Row becomes itself again – quiet and magical. Its normal life returns. The bums who retired in disgust under the black cypress-tree come out to sit on the rusty pipes in the vacant lot. The girls from Dora's emerge for a bit of sun if there is any. Doc strolls from the Western Biological Laboratory and crosses the street to Lee Chong's grocery for two quarts of beer. Henri the painter noses like an Airedale through the junk in the grass-grown lot for some part or piece of wood or metal he needs for the boat he is building. Then the darkness edges in and the street light comes on in front of Dora's – the lamp which makes perpetual moonlight in Cannery Row. Callers arrive at Western Biological to see Doc, and he crosses the street to Lee Chong's for five quarts of beer.

How can the poem and the stink and the grating noise – the quality of light, the tone, the habit and the dream – be set down alive? When you collect marine animals there are certain flat worms so delicate that they are almost impossible to capture whole, for they break and tatter under the touch. You must let them ooze and crawl of their own will on to a knife blade and then lift them gently into your bottle of sea water. And perhaps that might be the way to write this book – to open the page and to let the stories crawl in by themselves.

CHAPTER I

LEE CHONG's grocery, while not a model of neatness, was a miracle of supply. It was small and crowded but within its single room a man could find everything he needed or wanted to live and to be happy – clothes, food, both fresh and canned, liquor, tobacco, fishing equipment, machinery, boats, cordage, caps, pork-chops. You could buy at Lee Chong's a pair of slippers, a silk kimono, a quarter-pint of whisky, and a cigar. You could work out combinations to fit almost any mood. The one commodity Lee Chong did not keep could be had across the lot at Dora's.

The grocery opened at dawn and did not close until the last wandering vagrant dime had been spent or retired for the night. Not that Lee Chong was avaricious. He wasn't, but if one wanted to spend money, he was available. Lee's position in the community surprised him as much as he could be surprised. Over the course of the years everyone in Cannery Row owed him money. He never pressed his clients, but when the bill became too large, Lee cut off credit. Rather than walk into the town up the hill, the client usually paid or tried to.

Lee was round-faced and courteous. He spoke a stately English without ever using the letter R. When the tong wars were going on in California, it happened now and then that Lee found a price on his head. Then he would go secretly to San Francisco and enter a hospital until the trouble blew over. What he did with his money, no one ever knew. Perhaps he didn't get it. Maybe his wealth was entirely in unpaid bills. But he lived well and he had the respect of all his neighbours. He trusted his clients until further trust became ridiculous. Sometimes he made business errors, but even these he turned to advantage in good will if in no other way. It was that way with the Palace Flophouse and Grill. Any-one but Lee Chong would have considered the transaction a total loss.

Lee Chong's station in the grocery was behind the cigar counter. The cash register was then on his left and the abacus on his right. Inside the glass case were the brown cigars, the cigarettes, the Bull Durham, the Duke's mixture, the Five Brothers, while behind him in racks on the wall were the pints, half-pints, and quarters of Old Green River, Old Town House, Old Colonel, and the favourite – Old Tennessee, a blended whisky guaranteed four months old, very cheap and known in the neighbourhood as Old Tennis Shoes. Lee Chong did not stand between the whisky and the customer without reason. Some very practical minds had on occasion tried to divert his attention to another part of the store. Cousins, nephews, sons, and daughters-in-law waited on the rest of the store, but Lee never left the cigar counter. The top of the glass was his desk. His fat delicate hands rested on the glass, the fingers moving like small rest-less sausages. A broad golden wedding-ring on the middle finger of his left hand was his only jewellery and with it he silently tapped on the rubber change mat from which the little rubber tits had long been worn. Lee's mouth was full and benevolent and the flash of gold when he smiled was rich and warm. He wore half-glasses and since he looked at everything through them, he had to tilt his head back to see the distance. Interest and discounts, addition, subtraction he worked out on the abacus with his little restless sausage fingers, and his brown friendly eyes roved over the grocery and his teeth flashed at the customers.

On an evening when he stood in his place on a pad of newspaper to keep his feet warm, he contemplated with humour and sadness a business deal that had been consummated that afternoon and reconsummated later the same afternoon. When you leave the grocery, if you walk catty-cornered across the grass-grown lot, threading your way among the great rusty pipes thrown out of the canneries, you will see a path worn in the weeds. Follow it past the cypress-tree, across the railroad track, up a chicken-walk with cleats, and you will come to a long low building which for a long time was used as a storage place for fish meal. It was just a great big roofed room and it belonged to a worried gentleman name Horace Abbeville. Horace had two wives and six children, and over a period of years he had managed through pleading and persuasion to build a grocery debt second to none in Monterey. That afternoon he had come into the grocery and his sensitive tired face had flinched at the shadow of sternness that crossed Lee's face. Lee's fat finger tapped the rubber mat. Horace laid his hands palm up on the cigar counter. 'I guess I owe you plenty dough,' he said simply.

Lee's teeth flashed up in appreciation of an approach so different from any he had ever heard. He nodded gravely, but he waited for the trick to develop.

Horace wet his lips with his tongue, a good job from corner to corner. 'I hate to have my kids with that hanging over them,' he said. 'Why, I bet you wouldn't let them have a pack of spearmint now.'

Lee Chong's face agreed with this conclusion. 'Plenty dough,' he said.

Horace continued: 'You know that place of mine across the track up there where the fish meal is.'

Lee Chong nodded. It was his fish meal.

Horace said earnestly: 'If I was to give you that place – would it clear me up with you?'

Lee Chong tilted his head back and stared at Horace through his half-glasses while his mind flicked among accounts and his right hand moved restlessly to the abacus. He considered the construction which was flimsy and the lot which might be valuable if a cannery ever wanted to expand. 'Shu,' said Lee Chong.

'Well, get out the accounts and I'll make you a bill of sale on that place.' Horace seemed in a hurry.

'No need papers,' said Lee. 'I make paid-in-full paper.'

They finished the deal with dignity and Lee Chong threw in a quarter-pint of Old Tennis Shoes. And then Horace Abbeville walking very straight went across the lot and past the cypress-tree and across the track and up the chicken-walk and into the building that had been his, and he shot himself on a heap of fish meal. And although it has nothing to do with this story, no Abbeville child, no matter who its mother was, knew the lack of a stick of spearmint ever afterward.

But to get back to the evening. Horace was on the trestles with the embalming needles in him, and his two wives were sitting on the steps of his house with their arms about each other (they were good friends until after the funeral, and then they divided up the children and never spoke to each other again). Lee Chong stood behind the cigar counter and his nice brown eyes were turned inward on a calm and eternal Chinese sorrow. He knew he could not have helped it, but he wished he might have known and perhaps tried to help. It was deeply a part of Lee's kindness and understanding that man's right to kill himself is inviolable, but sometimes a friend can make it unnecessary. Lee had already underwritten the funeral and sent a wash-basket of groceries to the stricken families.

Now Lee Chong owned the Abbeville building – a good roof, a good floor, two windows and a door. True it was piled high with fish meal and the smell of it was delicate and penetrating. Lee Chong considered it as a storehouse for groceries, as a kind of warehouse, but he gave that up on second thought. It was too far away and anyone can go in through a window. He was tapping the rubber mat with his gold ring and considering the problem when the door opened and Mack came in. Mack was the elder, leader, mentor, and to a small extent the exploiter of a little group of men who had in common no families, no money, and no ambitions beyond food, drink, and contentment. But whereas most men in their search for contentment destroy themselves and fall wearily short of their targets, Mack and his friends approached contentment casually, quietly, and absorbed it gently. Mack and Hazel, a young man of great strength, Eddie who filled in as a bar-tender at La Ida, Hughie and Jones who occasionally collected frogs and cats for Western Biological, were currently living in those large rusty pipes in the lot next to Lee Chong's. That is, they lived in the pipes when it was damp, but in fine weather they lived in the shadow of the black cypress-tree at the top of the lot. The limbs folded down and made a canopy under which a man could lie and look out at the flow and vitality of Cannery Row.

Lee Chong stiffened ever so slightly when Mack came in and his eyes glanced quickly about the store to make sure that Eddie or Hazel or Hughie or Jones had not come in too and drifted away among the groceries.

Mack laid out his cards with a winning honesty. 'Lee,' he said, 'I and Eddie and the rest heard you own the Abbeville place.'

Lee Chong nodded and waited.

'I and my friends thought we'd ast you if we could move in there. We'll keep up the property,' he added quickly. 'Wouldn't let anybody break in or hurt anything. Kids might knock out the windows, you know ...' Mack suggested. 'Place might burn down if somebody don't keep an eye on it.'

Lee tilted his head back and looked into Mack's eyes through the half-glasses and Lee's tapping finger slowed its tempo as he thought deeply. In Mack's eyes there was good will and good fellowship and a desire to make everyone happy. Why then did Lee Chong feel slightly surrounded? Why did his mind pick its way as delicately as a cat through

cactus? It had been sweetly done, almost in a spirit of philanthropy. Lee's mind leaped ahead at the possibilities – no,
they were probabilities, and his finger tapping slowed still
further. He saw himself refusing Mack's request and he saw
the broken glass from the windows. Then Mack would offer
a second time to watch over and preserve Lee's property
and at the second refusal, Lee could smell the smoke, could
see the little flames creeping up the walls. Mack and his
friends would try to help to put it out. Lee's finger came to a
gentle rest on the change-mat. He was beaten. He knew
that. There was left to him only the possibility of saving
face, and Mack was likely to be very generous about that.
Lee said: 'You like pay lent my place? You like live there
same hotel?'

Mack smiled broadly and he was generous. 'Say . . .' he
cried. 'That's an idear. Sure. How much?'

Lee considered. He knew it didn't matter what he charged.
He wasn't going to get it, anyway. He might just as well make
it a really sturdy face-saving sum. 'Fi' dolla' week,' said Lee.

Mack played it through to the end. 'I'll have to talk to
the boys about it,' he said dubiously. 'Couldn't you make
that four dollars a week?'

'Fi' dolla',' said Lee firmly.

'Well, I'll see what the boys say,' said Mack.

And that was the way it was. Everyone was happy about
it. And if it be thought that Lee Chong suffered a total loss,
at least his mind did not work that way. The windows were
not broken. Fire did not break out, and while no rent was
ever paid, if the tenants ever had any money, and quite
often they did have, it never occurred to them to spend it
anywhere except at Lee Chong's grocery. What he had was
a little group of active and potential customers under wraps.
But it went further than that. If a drunk caused trouble in
the grocery, if the kids swarmed down from New Monterey
intent on plunder, Lee Chong had only to call and his
tenants rushed to his aid. One further bond it established –

you cannot steal from your benefactor. The saving to Lee Chong in cans of beans and tomatoes and milk and water-melons more than paid the rent. And if there was a sudden and increased leakage among the groceries in New Monterey that was none of Lee Chong's affair.

The boys moved in and the fish-meal moved out. No one knows who named the house that has been known ever after as the Palace Flophouse Grill. In the pipes and under the cypress-tree there had been no room for furniture and the little niceties which are not only the diagnoses but the boundaries of our civilization. Once in the Palace Flophouse, the boys set about furnishing it. A chair appeared and a cot and another chair. A hardware store supplied a can of red paint not reluctantly because it never knew about it, and as a new table or footstool appeared it was painted, which not only made it very pretty but also disguised it to a certain extent in case a former owner looked in. And the Palace Flophouse Grill began to function. The boys could sit in front of their door and look down across the track and across the lot and across the street right into the front windows of Western Biological. They could hear the music from the laboratory at night. And their eyes followed Doc across the street when he went to Lee Chong's for beer. And Mack said: 'That Doc is a fine fellow. We ought to do something for him.'

CHAPTER II

THE word is a symbol and a delight which sucks up men and scenes, trees, plants, factories, and Pekinese. Then the Thing becomes the Word and back to Thing again, but warped and woven into a fantastic pattern. The Word sucks up Cannery Row, digests it, and spews it out, and the Row has taken the shimmer of the green world and the sky-reflecting seas. Lee Chong is more than a Chinese grocer. He must be. Perhaps he is evil balanced and held suspended by good — an Asiatic planet held to its orbit by the pull of Lao Tze and held away from Lao Tze by the centrifugality of abacus and cash register — Lee Chong suspended, spin-ning, whirling among groceries and ghosts. A hard man with a can of beans — a soft man with the bones of his grand-father. For Lee Chong dug into the grave on China Point and found the yellow bones, the skull with grey ropy hair still sticking to it. And Lee carefully packed the bones, femurs, and tibias really straight, skull in the middle, with pelvis and clavicle surrounding it and ribs curving on either side. Then Lee Chong sent his boxed and brittle grandfather over the western sea to lie at last in ground made holy by his ancestors.

Mack and the boys, too, spinning in their orbits. They are the Virtues, the Graces, the Beauties of the hurried mangled craziness of Monterey and the cosmic Monterey where men in fear and hunger destroy their stomachs in the fight to secure certain food, where men hungering for love destroy everything lovable about them. Mack and the boys are the Beauties, the Virtues, the Graces. In the world ruled by tigers with ulcers, rutted by strictured bulls, scavenged by blind jackals, Mack and the boys dine delicately with the tigers, fondle the frantic heifers, and wrap up the crumbs to feed the sea-gulls of Cannery Row. What can it profit a man to gain the whole world and to come to his property with a gastric ulcer, a blown prostate, and bifocals? Mack and the boys avoid the trap, walk around the poison, step over the noose while a generation of trapped, poisoned, and trussed-up men scream at them and call them no-goods, come-to-bad-ends, blots-on-the-town, thieves, rascals, bums. Our Father who art in nature, who has given the gift of survival to the coyote, the common brown rat, the English sparrow, the house-fly, and the moth, must have a great and overwhelming love for no-goods and blots-on-the-town and bums, and Mack and the boys. Virtues and graces and laziness and zest. Our Father who art in nature.

CHAPTER III

LEE CHONG'S is to the right of the vacant lot (although why it is called vacant when it is piled high with old boilers, with rusting pipes, with great square timbers, and stacks of five-gallon cans, no one can say). In the rear of the vacant lot is the railroad track and the Palace Flophouse. But on the left-hand boundary of the lot is the stern and stately whore-house of Dora Flood; a decent, clean, honest, old-fashioned sporting house where a man can take a glass of beer among friends. This is no fly-by-night cheap clip-joint, but a sturdy, virtuous club, built, maintained, and disciplined by Dora, who, madam and girl for fifty years, has through the exercise of special gifts of tact and honesty, charity and a certain realism, made herself respected by the intelligent, the learned, and the kind. And by the same token she is hated by the twisted and lascivious sisterhood of married spinsters whose husbands respect the home but don't like it very much.

Dora is a great woman, a great big woman with flaming orange hair and a taste for Nile-green evening dresses. She keeps an honest, one-price house, sells no hard liquor, and permits no loud or vulgar talk in her house. Of her girls some are fairly inactive, due to age and infirmities, but Dora never puts them aside, although, as she says, some of them don't turn three tricks a month, but they go right on eating three meals a day. In a moment of local love Dora named her place the Bear Flag Restaurant and the stories are many of people who have gone in for a sandwich. There are normally twelve girls in the house, counting the old ones, a Greek cook, and a man who is known as a watchman, but who undertakes all manner of delicate and dangerous tasks. He stops fights, ejects drunks, soothes hysteria, cures headaches, and tends bar. He bandages cuts and bruises, passes the time of day with cops, and since a good half of the girls are Christian Scientists, reads aloud his share of *Science and Health* on a Sunday morning. His predecessor, being a less well-balanced man, came to an evil end as shall be reported, but Alfred has triumphed over his environment and has brought his environment up with him. He knows what men should be there and what men shouldn't be there. He knows more about the home life of Monterey citizens than anyone in town.

As for Dora – she leads a ticklish existence. Being against the law, at least against its letter, she must be twice as law-abiding as anyone else. There must be no drunks, no fighting, no vulgarity, or they close Dora up. Also being illegal Dora must be especially philanthropic. Everyone puts the bite on her. If the police give a dance for their pension fund and everyone else gives a dollar, Dora has to give fifty dollars. When the Chamber of Commerce improved its gardens, the merchants each gave five dollars, but Dora was asked for and gave a hundred. With everyone else it is the same, Red Cross, Community Chest, Boy Scouts, Dora's unsung, unpublicized, shameless dirty wages of sin lead the list of donations. But during the depression she was hardest hit. In addition to the usual charities, Dora saw the hungry children of Cannery Row and the jobless fathers and the worried women, and Dora paid grocery bills right and left for two years and very nearly went broke in the process. Dora's girls are well trained and pleasant. They never speak to a man on the street although he may have been in the night before.

Before Alfy, the present watchman, took over, there was a tragedy in the Bear Flag Restaurant which saddened everyone. The previous watchman was named William, and he was a dark and lonesome-looking man. In the day-time when his duties were few he would grow tired of female company. Through the windows he could see Mack and the boys sitting on the pipes in the vacant lot, dangling their feet in the mallow weeds and taking the sun while they discoursed slowly and philosophically of matters of interest but of no importance. Now and then as he watched them he saw them take out a pint of Old Tennis Shoes and wiping the neck of the bottle on a sleeve, raise the pint one after another. And William began to wish he could join that good group. He walked out one day and sat on the pipe. Conversation stopped and an uneasy and hostile silence fell on the group. After a while William went disconsolately back to the Bear Flag, and through the window he saw the conversation spring up again, and it saddened him. He had a dark and ugly face and a mouth twisted with brooding.

The next day he went again, and this time he took a pint of whisky. Mack and the boys drank the whisky, after all they weren't crazy, but all the talking they did was 'Good luck', and 'Lookin' at you'.

After a while William went back to the Bear Flag and he watched them through the window, and he heard Mack raise his voice saying: 'But God damn it, I hate a pimp!' Now this was obviously untrue, although William didn't know that. Mack and the boys just didn't like William.

Now William's heart broke. The bums would not receive him socially. They felt that he was too far beneath them. William had always been introspective and self-accusing. He put on his hat and walked out along the sea, clear out to the Lighthouse. And he stood in the pretty little cemetery where you can hear the waves drumming always. William thought dark and broody thoughts. No one loved him. No one cared about him. They might call him a watchman, but he was a pimp – a dirty pimp, the lowest thing in the world. And then he thought how he had a right to live and be happy just like anyone else, by God he had. He walked back angrily, but his anger went away when he came to the Bear Flag and climbed the steps. It was evening and the juke-box was playing *Harvest Moon* and William remembered that the first hooker who ever gaffed for him used to like that song before she ran away and got married and disappeared. The song made him awfully sad. Dora was in the back parlour having a cup of tea when William came in. She said: 'What's the matter, you sick?'

'No,' said William. 'But what's the percentage? I feel lousy. I think I'll bump myself off.'

Dora had handled plenty of neurotics in her time. Kid 'em out of it was her motto. 'Well, do it on your own time and don't mess up the rugs,' she said.

A grey damp cloud folded over William's heart and he walked slowly out and down the hall and knocked on Eva Flanagan's door. She had red hair and went to confession every week. Eva was quite a spiritual girl with a big family of brothers and sisters, but she was an unpredictable drunk. She was painting her nails and messing them pretty badly when William went in and he knew she was bagged and Dora wouldn't let a bagged girl work. Her fingers were nail polish to the first joint and she was angry. 'What's eating you?' she said. William grew angry too. 'I'm going to bump myself off,' he said fiercely.

Eva screeched at him. 'That's a dirty, lousy, stinking sin,' she cried, and then: 'Wouldn't it be like you to get the joint pinched just when I got almost enough kick to take a trip to East St Louis. You're a no-good bastard.' She was still screaming at him when William shut her door after him and went to the kitchen. He was very tired of women. The Greek would be restful after women.

The Greek, big apron, sleeves rolled up, was frying pork-chops in two big skillets, turning them over with an ice-pick. 'Hello, Kits. How is going things?' The pork-chops hissed and swished in the pan.

'I don't know, Lou,' said William. 'Sometimes I think the best thing to do would be – kluck!' He drew his finger across his throat.

The Greek laid the ice-pick on the stove and rolled his sleeves higher. 'I tell you what I hear, Kits,' he said. 'I hear like the fella talks about it don't never do it.' William's hand went out for the ice-pick and he held it easily in his hand. His eyes looked deeply into the Greek's dark eyes, and he saw disbelief and amusement, and then as he stared the Greek's eyes grew troubled and then worried. And William saw the change, saw first how the Greek knew he could do it and then the Greek knew he would do it. As soon as he saw that in the Greek's eyes William knew he had to do it. He was sad because now it seemed silly. His hand rose and the ice-pick snapped into his heart. It was amazing how easily it went in. William was the watchman before Alfred came. Everyone liked Alfred. He could sit on the pipes with Mack and the boys any time. He could even visit up at the Palace Flophouse.

CHAPTER IV

In the evening just at dusk, a curious thing happened on Cannery Row. It happened in the time between sunset and the lighting of the street light. There is a small quiet grey period then. Down the hill, past the Palace Flophouse, down the chicken-walk, and through the vacant lot came an old Chinaman. He wore an ancient flat straw hat, blue jeans, both coat and trousers, and heavy shoes of which one sole was loose so that it slapped the ground when he walked. In his hand he carried a covered wicker-basket. His face was lean and brown and corded as jerky and his old eyes were brown, even the whites were brown and deep-set so that they looked out of holes. He came by just at dusk and crossed the street and went through the opening between Western Biological and the Hediondo Cannery. Then he crossed the little beach and disappeared among the piles and steel posts which support the piers. No one saw him again until dawn.

But in the dawn, during that time when the street light has been turned off and the daylight has not come, the old Chinaman crept out from among the piles, crossed the beach and the street. His wicker-basket was heavy and wet and dropping now. His loose sole flap-flapped on the street. He went up the hill to the second street, went through a gate in a high board fence, and was not seen again until evening. People, sleeping, heard his flapping shoe go by and they awakened for a moment. It had been happening for years, but no one ever got used to him. Some people thought he was God and very old people thought he was Death and children thought he was a very funny old Chinaman, as children always think anything old and strange is funny. But the children did not taunt him or shout at him as they should, for he carried a little cloud of fear about with him.

Only one brave and beautiful boy of ten named Andy from Salinas ever crossed the old Chinaman. Andy was visiting in Monterey and he saw the old man and knew he must shout at him if only to keep his self-respect, but even Andy, brave as he was, felt the little cloud of fear. Andy watched him go by evening after evening, while his duty and his terror wrestled. And then one evening Andy braced himself and marched behind the old man singing in a shrill falsetto: 'Ching-Chong Chinaman sitting on a rail – 'Long came a white man an' chopped off his tail.'

The old man stopped and turned. Andy stopped. The

deep-brown eyes looked at Andy and the thin corded lips moved. What happened then Andy was never able either to explain or to forget. For the eyes spread out until there was no Chinaman. And then it was one eye – one huge brown eye as big as a church door. Andy looked through the shiny transparent brown door and through it he saw a lonely countryside, flat for miles but ending against a row of fantastic mountains shaped like cows' and dogs' heads and tents and mushrooms. There was low coarse grass on the plain and here and there a little mound. And a small animal like a woodchuck sat on each mound. And the loneliness – the desolate cold aloneness of the landscape made Andy whimper because there wasn't anybody at all in the world and he was left. Andy shut his eyes so he wouldn't have to see it any more and when he opened them, he was in Cannery Row and the old Chinaman was just flip-flapping between Western Biological and the Hediondo Cannery. Andy was the only boy who ever did that and he never did it again.

CHAPTER V

WESTERN BIOLOGICAL was right across the street and facing the vacant lot. Lee Chong's grocery was on its catty-corner right and Dora's Bear Flag Restaurant was on its catty-corner left. Western Biological deals in strange and beautiful wares. It sells the lovely animals of the sea, the sponges, tunicates, anemones, the stars and buttlestars, and sun stars, the bivalves, barnacles, the worm and shells, the fabulous and multiform little brothers, the living moving flowers of the sea, nudibranchs and ectibranchs, the spiked and nobbed and needy urchins, the crabs and demi-crabs, the little dragoons, the snapping shrimps, and ghost shrimps so transparent that they hardly throw a shadow. And Western Biological sells bugs and snails and spiders, and rattlesnakes, and rats, and honey bees and gila monsters. These are all for sale. Then there are little unborn humans, some whole and others sliced thin and mounted on slides. And for students there are sharks with the blood drained out and yellow and blue colour substituted in veins and arteries, so that you may follow the systems with a scalpel. And there are cats with coloured veins and arteries, and frogs the same. You can order anything living from Western Biological and sooner or later you will get it.

It is a low building facing the street. The basement is the store-room with shelves, shelves clear to the ceiling, loaded with jars of preserved animals. And in the basement is a sink and instrument for embalming and for injecting. Then you go through the backyard to a covered shed on piles over the ocean and here are the tanks for the larger animals, the sharks and rays and octopi, each in their concrete tanks. There is a stairway up the front of the building and a door that opens into an office where there is a desk piled high with unopened mail, filing cabinets, and a safe with the door propped open. Once the safe got locked by mistake and no one knew the combination. And in the safe was an open can of sardines and a piece of Roquefort cheese. Before the combination could be sent by the maker of the lock, there was trouble in the safe. It was then that Doc devised a method for getting revenge on a bank if anyone should ever want to. 'Rent a safety-deposit box,' he said, 'then deposit in it one whole fresh salmon and go away for six months.' After the trouble with the safe, it was not permitted to keep food there any more. It is kept in the filing cabinets. Behind the office is a room where in aquaria are many living animals; there are also the microscopes and the slides and the drug cabinets, the cases of laboratory glass, the work benches and little motors, the chemicals. From this room comes smells – formaline, and dry starfish, and sea water and menthol, carbolic acid and acetic acid, smell of brown wrapping-paper and straw and rope, smell of chloroform and ether, smell of ozone from the motors, smell of fine steel and thin lubricant from the microscopes, smell of banana oil and rubber tubing, smell of drying wool socks and boots, sharp pungent smell of rattlesnakes, and musty frightening smell of rats. And through the back door comes the smell of kelp and barnacles when the tide is out and the smell of salt and spray when the tide is in.

To the left the office opens into a library. The walls are bookcases to the ceiling, boxes of pamphlets and separates books of all kinds, dictionaries, encyclopaedias, poetry, plays. A great phonograph stands against the wall with hundreds of records lined up beside it. Under the window is a red-wood bed and on the walls and to the bookcases are pinned reproductions of Daumiers, and Graham, Titian, and Leonardo and Picasso, Dali and George Grosz, pinned here and there at eye level, so that you can look at them if you want to. There are chairs and benches in this little room and of course, the bed. As many as forty people have been here at one time.

Behind this library or music-room, or whatever you want to call it, is the kitchen, a narrow chamber with a gas-stove, a water-heater, and a sink. But whereas some food is kept in the filing cabinets in the office, dishes and cooking fat and vegetables are kept in glass-fronted sectional bookcases in the kitchen. No whimsy dictated this. It just happened. From the ceiling of the kitchen hang pieces of bacon, and salami, and black bêche-de-mer. Behind the kitchen is a toilet and a shower. The toilet leaked for five years until a clever and handsome guest fixed it with a piece of chewing-gum.

Doc is the owner and operator of the Western Biological Laboratory. Doc is rather small, deceptively small, for he is wiry and very strong and when passionate anger comes on him he can be very fierce. He wears a beard and his face is half Christ and half satyr and his face tells the truth. It is said that he has helped many a girl out of one trouble and into another. Doc has the hands of a brain surgeon, and a cool warm mind. Doc tips his hat to dogs as he drives by and the dogs look up and smile at him. He can kill anything for need, but he could not even hurt a feeling for pleasure. He has one great fear – that of getting his head wet, so that summer or winter he ordinarily wears a rain hat. He will wade in a tide pool up to the chest without feeling damp, but a drop of rain water on his head makes him panicky.

Over a period of years Doc dug himself into Cannery Row to an extent not even he suspected. He became the fountain of philosophy and science and art. In the laboratory the girls from Dora's heard the Plain Songs and Gregorian music for the first time. Lee Chong listened while Li Po was read to him in English. Henri the painter heard for the first time the Book of the Dead and was so moved that he changed his medium. Henri had been painting with glue, iron rust, and coloured chicken feathers, but he changed and his next four paintings were done entirely with different kinds of nutshells. Doc would listen to any kind of nonsense and change it for you to a kind of wisdom. His mind had no horizon – and his sympathy had no warp. He could talk to children, telling them very profound things so that they understood. He lived in a world of wonders, of excitement. He was concupiscent as a rabbit and gentle as hell. Everyone who knew him was indebted to him. And everyone who thought of him thought next: 'I really must do something nice for Doc.'

CHAPTER VI

Doc was collecting marine animals in the Great Tide Pool on the tip of the Peninsula. It is a fabulous place; when the tide is in, a wave-churned basin, creamy with foam, whipped by the combers that roll in from the whistling buoy on the reef. But when the tide goes out the little water world becomes quiet and lovely. The sea is very clear and the bottom becomes fantastic with hurrying, fighting, feeding, breeding animals. Crabs rush from frond to frond of the waving algae. Starfish squat over mussels and limpets, attach their million little suckers and then slowly lift with incredible power until the prey is broken from the rock. And then the starfish stomach comes out and envelops its food. Orange and speckled and fluted nudibranchs slide gracefully over the rocks, their skirts waving like the dresses of Spanish dancers. And black eels poke their heads out of crevices and wait for prey. The snapping shrimps with their trigger claws pop loudly. The lovely, coloured world is glassed over. Hermit crabs like frantic children scamper on the bottom sand. And now one, finding an empty snail shell he likes better than his own, creeps out, exposing his soft body to the enemy for a moment, and then pops into the new shell. A wave breaks over the barrier, and churns the glassy water for a moment and mixes bubbles into the pool, and then it clears and is tranquil and lovely and murderous again. Here a crab tears a leg from his brother. The anemones expand like soft and brilliant flowers, inviting any tired and perplexed animal to lie for a moment in their arms, and when some small crab or little tide-pool Johnnie accepts the green and purple invitation, the petals whip in, the stinging cells shoot tiny narcotic needles into the prey and it grows weak and perhaps sleepy while the searing caustic digestive acids melt its body down.

Then the creeping murderer, the octopus, steals out, slowly, softly, moving like a grey mist, pretending now to be a bit of weed, now a rock, now lump of decaying meat, while its evil goat eyes watch coldly. It oozes and flows toward a feeding crab, and as it comes close its yellow eyes burn and its body turns rosy with the pulsing colour of anticipation and rage. Then suddenly it runs lightly on the tip of its arms, as ferociously as a charging cat. It leaps savagely on the crab, there is a puff of black fluid, and the struggling mass is obscured in the sepia cloud while the octopus murders the crab. On the exposed rocks out of water, the barnacles bubble behind their closed doors and the limpets dry out. And down to the rocks come the black flies to eat anything they can find. The sharp smell of iodine from the algae, and the lime smell of calcareous bodies and the smell of powerful protean, smell of sperm and ova fill the air. On the exposed rocks the starfish emit semen and eggs from between their rays. The smells of life and richness, of death and digestion, of decay and birth, burden the air. And salt spray blows in from the barrier where the ocean waits for its rising-tide strength to permit it back into the Great Tide Pool again. And on the reef the whistling buoy bellows like a sad and patient bull.

In the pool Doc and Hazel worked together. Hazel lived in the Palace Flophouse with Mack and the boys. Hazel got his name in as haphazard a way as his life was ever afterward. His worried mother had had seven children in eight years. Hazel was the eighth, and his mother became confused about his sex when he was born. She was tired and run down anyway from trying to feed and clothe seven children and their father. She had tried every possible way of making money – paper flowers, mushrooms at home, rabbits for meat and fur – while her husband from a canvas chair gave her every help his advice and reasoning and criticism could offer. She had a great aunt named Hazel who was reputed to carry life insurance. The eighth child was named Hazel before the mother got it through her head that Hazel was a boy and by that time she was used to the name and never bothered to change it. Hazel grew up – did four years in grammar school, four years in reform school, and didn't learn anything in either place. Reform schools are supposed to teach viciousness and criminality, but Hazel didn't pay enough attention. He came out of reform school as innocent of viciousness as he was of fractions and long division. Hazel loved to hear conversation but he didn't listen to words – just to the tone of conversation. He asked questions, not to hear the answers but simply to continue the flow. He was twenty-six – dark-haired and pleasant, strong, willing and loyal. Quite often he went collecting with Doc and he was very good at it once he knew what was wanted. His fingers would creep like an octopus, could grab and hold like an anemone. He was sure-footed on the slippery rocks and he loved the hunt. Doc wore his rain hat and high rubber-boots as he worked, but Hazel sloshed about in tennis-shoes and blue jeans. They were collecting starfish. Doc had an order for three hundred.

Hazel picked a nobby purplish starfish from the bottom of the pool and popped it into his nearly-full gunny sack. 'I wonder what they do with them,' he said.

'Do with what?' Doc asked.

'The starfish,' said Hazel. 'You sell 'em. You'll send out a barrel of 'em. What do the guys do with 'em? You can't eat 'em.'

'They study them,' said Doc patiently and he remembered that he had answered this question for Hazel dozens of times before. But Doc had one mental habit he could not get over. When anyone asked a question, Doc thought he wanted to know the answer. That was the way with Doc.

He never asked unless he wanted to know and he could not conceive of the brain that would ask without wanting to know. But Hazel, who simply wanted to hear talk, had developed a system of making the answer to one question the basis of another. It kept conversation going.

'What do they find to study?' Hazel continued. 'They're just starfish. There's millions of 'em around. I could get you a million of 'em.'

'They're complicated and interesting animals,' Doc said a little defensively. 'Besides, these are going to the Middle West to Northwestern University.'

Hazel used his trick. 'They got no starfish there?'

'They got no ocean there,' said Doc.

'Oh!' said Hazel and he cast frantically about for a peg to hang a new question on. He hated to have a conversation die out like this. He wasn't quick enough. While he was looking for a question Doc asked one. Hazel hated that, it meant casting about in his mind for an answer and casting about in Hazel's mind was like wandering alone in a deserted museum. Hazel's mind was choked with uncatalogued exhibits. He never forgot anything, but he never bothered to arrange his memories. Everything was thrown together like fishing-tackle in the bottom of a rowboat, hooks and sinkers and line and lures and gaffs all snarled up.

Doc asked: 'How are things going up at the Palace?'

Hazel ran his fingers through his dark hair and he peered into the clutter of his mind. 'Pretty good,' he said. 'That fellow Gay is moving in with us, I guess. His wife hits him pretty bad. He don't mind that when he's awake, but she waits 'til he gets to sleep and then hits him. He hates that. He has to wake up and beat her up and then when he goes back to sleep she hits him again. He don't get any rest, so he's moving in with us.'

'That's a new one,' said Doc. 'She used to swear out a warrant and put him in jail.'

'Yeah!' said Hazel. 'But that was before they built the

new jail in Salinas. Used to be thirty days and Gay was pretty hot to get out, but this new jail – radio in the tank and good bunks and the sheriff's a nice fellow. Gay gets in there and he don't want to come out. He likes it so much his wife won't get him arrested any more. So she figured out this hitting him while he's asleep. It's nerve racking, he says. And you know as good as me – Gay never did take any pleasure in beating her up. He only done it to keep his self-respect. But he gets tired of it. I guess he'll be with us now.'

Doc straightened up. The waves were beginning to break over the barrier of the Great Tide Pool. The tide was coming in and little rivers from the sea had begun to flow over the rocks. The wind blew freshly in from the whistling buoy and the barking sea-lions came from round the point. Doc pushed his rain hat on the back of his head. 'We've got enough starfish,' he said and then went on: 'Look, Hazel, I know you've got six or seven undersized abalones in the bottom of your sack. If we get stopped by a game warden, you're going to say they're mine, on my permit – aren't you?'

'Well – hell,' said Hazel.

'Look,' Doc said kindly. 'Suppose I get an order for abalones and maybe the game warden thinks I'm using my collecting permit too often. Suppose he thinks I'm eating them.'

'Well – hell,' said Hazel.

'It's like the industrial alcohol board. They've got suspicious minds. They always think I'm drinking the alcohol. They think that about everyone.'

'Well, ain't you?'

'Not much of it,' said Doc. 'That stuff they put in it tastes terrible and it's a big job to re-distil it.'

'That stuff ain't so bad,' said Hazel. 'Me and Mack had a snort at it the other day. What is it they put in?'

Doc was about to answer when he saw it was Hazel's trick again. 'Let's get moving,' he said. He hoisted his sack of starfish on his shoulder. And he had forgotten the illegal abalones in the bottom of Hazel's sack.

Hazel followed him up out of the tide pool and up the slippery trail to solid ground. The little crabs scampered and skittered out of their way. Hazel felt that he had better cement the grave over the topic of the abalones.

'That painter guy came back to the Palace,' he offered.

'Yes?' said Doc.

'Yeah! You see, he done all our pictures in chicken-feathers and now he says he got to do them all over again with nut-shells. He says he changed his – his med – medium.'

Doc chuckled. 'He still building his boat?'

'Sure,' said Hazel. 'He's got it all changed around. New kind of a boat. I guess he'll take it apart and change it. Doc – is he nuts?'

Doc swung his heavy sack of starfish to the ground and stood panting a little. 'Nuts?' he asked. 'Oh, yes, I guess so. Nuts about the same amount we are, only in a different way.'

Such a thing had never occurred to Hazel. He looked upon himself as a crystal pool of clarity and on his life as a troubled glass of misunderstood virtue. Doc's last statement had outraged him a little. 'But the boat . . .' he cried. 'He's been building that boat for seven years that I know of. The blocks rotted out and he made concrete blocks. Every time he gets it nearly finished he changes it and starts over again. I think he's nuts. Seven years on a boat.'

Doc was sitting on the ground pulling off his rubber boots. 'You don't understand,' he said gently. 'Henri loves boats, but he's afraid of the ocean.'

'What's he want a boat for then?' Hazel demanded.

'He likes boats,' said Doc. 'But suppose he finishes his boat. Once it's finished people will say: "Why don't you put it in the water?" Then if he puts it in the water, he'll have to go out in it, and he hates the water. So you see, he never finishes the boat – so he doesn't ever have to launch it.'

Hazel had followed this reasoning to a certain point, but he abandoned it before it was resolved, not only abandoned it but searched for some way to change the subject. 'I think he's nuts,' he said lamely.

On the black earth on which the ice-plants bloomed hundreds of black stink bugs crawled. And many of them stuck their tails up in the air. 'Look at all them stink bugs,' Hazel remarked, grateful to the bugs for being there.

'They're interesting,' said Doc.

'Well, what they got their asses up in the air for?'

Doc rolled up his wool socks and put them in the rubber-boots and from his pocket he brought out dry socks and a pair of thin moccasins. 'I don't know why,' he said. 'I looked them up recently – they're very common animals and one of the commonest things they do is put their tails up in the air. And in all the books there isn't one mention of the fact that they put their tails up in the air or why.'

Hazel turned one of the stink bugs over with the toe of his wet tennis-shoe and the shining black beetle strove madly with floundering legs to get upright again. 'Well, why do *you* think they do it?'

'I think they're praying,' said Doc.

'What!' Hazel was shocked.

'The remarkable thing,' said Doc, 'isn't that they put their tails up in the air – the really incredibly remarkable thing is that we find it remarkable. We can only use ourselves as yardsticks. If we did something as inexplicable and strange we'd probably be praying – so maybe they're praying.'

'Let's get the hell out of here,' said Hazel.

CHAPTER VII

THE Palace Flophouse was no sudden development. Indeed when Mack and Hazel and Eddie and Hughie and Jones moved into it, they looked upon it as little more than shelter from the wind and the rain, as a place to go when everything else had closed or when their welcome was thin and sere with over-use. Then the Palace was only a long bare room, lit dimly by two small windows, walled with unpainted wood smelling strongly of fish meal. They had not loved it then. But Mack knew that some kind of organization was necessary, particularly among such a group of ravening individualists.

A training army which has not been equipped with guns and artillery and tanks uses artificial guns and masquerading trucks to simulate its destructive panoply – and its toughening soldiers get used to field-guns by handling logs on wheels.

Mack, with a piece of chalk, drew five oblongs on the floor, each seven feet long and four feet wide, and in each square he wrote a name. These were the simulated beds. Each man had property rights inviolable in his space. He could legally fight a man who encroached on his square. The rest of the room was property common to all. That was in the first days when Mack and the boys sat on the floor, played cards hunkered down, and slept on the hard boards. Perhaps, save for an accident of weather, they might always have lived that way. However, an unprecedented rainfall which went on for over a month changed all that. House-ridden, the boys grew tired of squatting on the floor. Their eyes became outraged by the bare board walls. Because it sheltered them the house grew dear to them. And it had the charm of never knowing the entrance of an outraged landlord. For Lee Chong never came near it. Then one afternoon Hughie came in with an army cot which had a torn canvas. He spent two hours sewing up the rip with fishingline. And that night the others lying on the floor in their squares watched Hughie ooze gracefully into his cot – they heard him sigh with abysmal comfort and he was asleep and snoring before anyone else.

The next day Mack puffed up the hill carrying a rusty set of springs he had found on a scrap-iron dump. The apathy was broken then. The boys outdid one another in beautifying the Palace Flophouse until after a few months it was, if anything, over-furnished. There were old carpets on the floor, chairs with and without seats. Mack had a wicker chaise-longue painted bright red. There were tables, a grandfather clock without dial face or works. The walls were whitewashed, which made it almost light and airy. Pictures began to appear – mostly calendars showing improbable luscious blondes holding bottles of Coca-Cola. Henri had contributed two pieces from his chicken-feather period. A bundle of gilded cat-tails stood in one corner and a sheaf of peacock-feathers was nailed to the wall beside the grandfather clock.

They were some time acquiring a stove and when they did find what they wanted, a silver-scrolled monster with floriated warming ovens and a front like a nickle-plated tulip garden, they had trouble getting it. It was too big to steal and its owner refused to part with it to the sick widow with eight children whom Mack invented and patronized in the same moment. The owner wanted a dollar and a half and didn't come down to eighty cents for three days. The boys closed at eighty cents and gave him an I O U, which he probably still has. This transaction took place in Seaside and the stove weighed three hundred pounds. Mack and

Hughie exhausted every possibility of haulage for ten days and only when they realized that no one was going to take this stove home for them did they begin to carry it. It took them three days to carry it to Cannery Row, a distance of five miles, and they camped beside it at night. But once installed in the Palace Flophouse it was the glory and the heart and the centre. Its nickel flowers and foliage shone with a cheery light. It was the gold tooth of the Palace. Fired up, it warmed the big room. Its oven was wonderful and you could fry an egg on its shiny black lids.

With the great stove came pride, and with pride, the Palace became home. Eddie planted morning glories to run over the door and Hazel acquired some rather rare fuchsia-bushes planted in five gallon cans which made the entrance formal and a little cluttered. Mack and the boys loved the Palace and they even cleaned it a little sometimes. In their minds they sneered at unsettled people who had no house to go to and occasionally in their pride they brought a guest home for a day or two.

Eddie was understudy bar-tender at 'La Ida'. He filled in when Whitey the regular bar-tender was sick, which was as often as Whitey could get away with it. Every time Eddie filled in, a few bottles disappeared, so he couldn't fill in too often. But Whitey liked to have Eddie take his place because he was convinced, and correctly, that Eddie was one man who wouldn't try to keep his job permanently. Almost anyone could have trusted Eddie to this extent. Eddie didn't have to remove much liquor. He kept a gallon jug under the bar and in the mouth of the jug there was a funnel. Anything left in the glasses Eddie poured into the funnel before he washed the glasses. If an argument or a song were going on at 'La Ida', or late at night when good fellowship had reached its logical conclusion, Eddie poured glasses half- or two-thirds full into the funnel. The resulting punch which he took back to the Palace was always interesting and some-times surprising. The mixture of rye, beer, bourbon, Scotch, wine, rum, and gin was fairly constant, but now and then some effete customer would order a stinger or an anisette or a curaçao and these little touches gave a distinct character to the punch. It was Eddie's habit always to shake a little Angostura into the jug before he left. On a good night Eddie got three-quarters of a gallon. It was a source of satisfaction to him that nobody was out anything. He had observed that a man got just as drunk on half a glass as on a whole one, that is, if he was in the mood to get drunk at all.

Eddie was a very desirable inhabitant of the Palace Flophouse. The others never asked him to help with the house-cleaning and once Hazel washed four pairs of Eddie's socks.

Now on the afternoon when Hazel was out collecting with Doc in the Great Tide Pool, the boys were sitting around in the Palace sipping the result of Eddie's latest contribution. Gay was there too, the latest member of the group. Eddie sipped speculatively from his glass and smacked his lips. 'It's funny how you get a run,' he said. 'Take last night. There was at least ten guys ordered Manhattans. Sometimes maybe you don't get two calls for a Manhattan in a month. It's the grenadine gives the stuff that taste.'

Mack tasted his – a big taste – and refilled his glass. 'Yes,' he said sombrely, 'it's little things make the difference.' He looked about to see how this gem had set with the others.

Only Gay got the full impact. 'Sure is,' he said. 'Does . . .'

'Where's Hazel today?' Mack asked.

Jones said: 'Hazel went out with Doc to get some starfish.'

Mack nodded his head soberly. 'That Doc is a hell of a nice fella,' he said. 'He'll give you a quarter any time. When I cut myself he put on a new bandage every day. A hell of a nice fella.'

The others nodded in profound agreement.

'I been wondering for a long time,' Mack continued,

'what we could do for him – something nice. Something he'd like.'

'He'd like a dame,' said Hughie.

'He's got three four dames,' said Jones. 'You can always tell – when he pulls them front curtains closed and when he plays that kind of church music on the phonograph.'

Mack said reprovingly to Hughie: 'Just because he doesn't run no dame naked through the streets in the daytime, you think Doc's celebrate.'

'What's celebrate?' Eddie asked.

'That's when you can't get no dame,' said Mack.

'I thought it was a kind of party,' said Jones.

A silence fell on the room. Mack shifted in his chaiselongue. Hughie let the front legs of his chair down on the floor. They looked into space and then they all looked at Mack. Mack said: 'Hum!'

Eddie said: 'What kind of a party you think Doc'd like?'

'What other kind is there?' said Jones.

Mack mused: 'Doc wouldn't like this stuff from the winin' jug.'

'How do you know?' Hughie demanded. 'You never offered him none.'

'Oh, I know,' said Mack. 'He's been to college. Once I seen a dame in a fur coat go in there. Never did see her come out. It was two o'clock the last I looked – and that church music goin'. No – you couldn't offer him none of this.' He filled his glass again.

'This tastes pretty nice after the third glass,' Hughie said loyally.

'No,' said Mack. 'Not for Doc. Have to be whisky – the real thing.'

'He likes beer,' said Jones. 'He's all the time going over to Lee's for beer – sometimes in the middle of the night.'

Mack said: 'I figure when you buy beer, you're buying too much tare. Take 8 per cent beer – why you're spending your dough for 92 per cent water and colour and hops and stuff like that. Eddie,' he added, 'you think you could get four five bottles of whisky at "La Ida" next time Whitey's sick?'

'Sure,' said Eddie. 'Sure I could get it, but that'd be the end – no more golden eggs. I think Johnnie's suspicious anyways. Other day he says: "I smell a mouse named Eddie." I was gonna lay low and only bring the jug for a while.'

'Yeah!' said Jones. 'Don't you lose that job. If something happened to Whitey, you could fall right in there for a week or so 'til they got somebody else. I guess if we're goin' to give a party for Doc, we got to buy the whisky. How much is whisky a gallon?'

'I don't know,' said Hughie. 'I never get more than a half-pint at a time myself – at one time that is. I figure you get a quart and right away you got friends. But you get a half-pint and you can drink it in the lot before – well before you got a lot of folks around.'

'It's going to take dough to give Doc a party,' said Mack. 'If we're going to give him a party at all it ought to be a good one. Should have a big cake. I wonder when is his birthday?'

'Don't need a birthday for a party,' said Jones.

'No – but it's nice,' said Mack. 'I figure it would take ten or twelve bucks to give Doc a party you wouldn't be ashamed of.'

They looked at one another speculatively. Hughie suggested: 'The Hediondo Cannery is hiring guys.'

'No,' said Mack quickly. 'We got good reputations and we don't want to spoil them. Every one of us keeps a job for a month or more when we take one. That's why we can always get a job when we need one. S'pose we take a job for a day or so – why we'll lose our reputation for sticking. Then if we needed a job there wouldn't nobody have us.' The rest nodded quick agreement.

'I figure I'm gonna work a couple of months – November and part of December,' said Jones. 'Makes it nice to have money around Christmas. We could cook a turkey this year.'

'By God, we could,' said Mack. 'I know a place up Carmel Valley where there's fifteen hundred in one flock.'

'Valley,' said Hughie. 'You know I used to collect stuff up the Valley for Doc, turtles and crayfish and frogs. Got a nickel apiece for frogs.'

'Me, too,' said Gay. 'I got five hundred frogs one time.'

'If Doc needs frogs it's a set-up,' said Mack. 'We could go up the Carmel River and have a little outing and we wouldn't tell Doc what it was for and then we'd give him one hell of a party.'

A quiet excitement grew in the Palace Flophouse. 'Gay,' said Mack, 'take a look out the door and see if Doc's car is in front of his place.'

Gay set down his glass and looked out. 'Not yet,' he said.

'Well, he ought to be back any minute,' said Mack. 'Now here's how we'll go about it . . .'

CHAPTER VIII

In April 1932, the boiler at the Hediondo Cannery blew a tube for the third time in two weeks and the board of directors, consisting of Mr Randolph and a stenographer, decided that it would be cheaper to buy a new boiler than to have to shut down so often. In time the new boiler arrived and the old one was moved into the vacant lot between Lee Chong's and the Bear Flag Restaurant, where it was set on blocks to await an inspiration on Mr Randolph's part on how to make some money out of it. Gradually, the plant engineer removed the tubing to use to patch other out-worn equipment at the Hediondo. The boiler looked like an old-fashioned locomotive without wheels. It had a big door in the centre of its nose and a low fire door. Gradually, it became red and soft with rust and gradually the mallow weeds grew up around it and the flaking rust fed the weeds. Flowering myrtle crept up its sides and the wild anise perfumed the air about it. Then someone threw out a datura root and the thick fleshy tree grew up and the great white bells hung over the boiler door and at night the flowers smelled of love and excitement, an incredibly sweet and moving odour.

In 1935 Mr and Mrs Sam Malloy moved into the boiler. The tubing was all gone now and it was a roomy, dry and safe apartment. True, if you came in through the fire door you had to get down on your hands and knees, but once in there was head room in the middle and you couldn't want a dryer, warmer place to stay. They shagged a mattress through the fire door and settled down. Mr Malloy was happy and contented there and for quite a long time so was Mrs Malloy.

Below the boiler on the hill there were numbers of large pipes also abandoned by the Hediondo. Toward the end of 1937 there was a great catch of fish and the canneries were working full time and a housing shortage occurred. Then it was that Mr Malloy took to renting the larger pipes as sleeping-quarters for single men at a very nominal fee. With a piece of tar paper over one end and a square of carpet over the other, they made comfortable bedrooms, although men used to sleeping curled up had to change their habits or move out. There were those too who claimed that their snores echoing back from the pipes woke them up. But on the whole Mr Malloy did a steady small business and was happy.

Mrs Malloy had been contented until her husband became a landlord and then she began to change. First it was a rug, then a wash-tub, then a lamp with a coloured silk shade. Finally, she came into the boiler on her hands and knees one day and she stood up and said a little breath-lessly: 'Holman's are having a sale of curtains. Real lace curtains and edges of blue and pink – $1.98 a set with curtain rods thrown in.'

Mr Malloy sat up on the mattress. 'Curtains?' he de-manded. 'What in God's name do you want curtains for?'

'I like things nice,' said Mrs Malloy. 'I always did like to have things nice for you,' and her lower lip began to tremble.

'But, darling,' Sam Malloy cried, 'I got nothing against curtains. I like curtains.'

'Only $1.98,' Mrs Malloy quavered, 'and you begrutch me $1.98,' and she sniffled and her chest heaved.

'I don't begrutch you,' said Mr Malloy. 'But, darling – for Christ's sake what are we going to do with curtains? We got no windows.'

Mrs Malloy cried and cried and Sam held her in his arms and comforted her.

'Men just don't understand how a woman feels,' she sobbed. 'Men just never try to put themselves in a woman's place.'

And Sam lay beside her and rubbed her back for a long time before she went to sleep.

CHAPTER IX

When Doc's car came back to the laboratory, Mack and the boys secretly watched Hazel help to carry in the sacks of starfish. In a few minutes Hazel came damply up the chicken-walk to the Palace. His jeans were wet with sea water to the thighs and where it was drying the white salt rings were forming. He sat heavily in the patient rocker that was his and shucked off his wet tennis shoes.

Mack asked: 'How is Doc feeling?'

'Fine,' said Hazel. 'You can't understand a word he says. Know what he said about stink bugs? No – I better not tell you.'

'He seem in a nice friendly mood?' Mack asked.

'Sure,' said Hazel. 'We got two three hundred starfish. He's all right.'

'I wonder if we better all go over?' Mack asked himself and he answered himself: 'No, I guess it would be better if one went alone. It might get him mixed up if we all went.'

'What is this?' Hazel asked.

'We got plans,' said Mack. 'I'll go myself so as not to startle him. You guys stay here and wait. I'll come back in a few minutes.'

Mack went out and he teetered down the chicken-walk and across the track. Mr Malloy was sitting on a brick in front of his boiler.

'How are you, Sam?' Mack asked.

'Pretty good.'

'How's the missus?'

'Pretty good,' said Mr Malloy. 'You know any kind of glue that you can stick cloth to iron?'

Ordinarily, Mack would have thrown himself headlong into this problem, but now he was not to be deflected. 'No,' he said.

He went across the vacant lot, crossed the street, and entered the basement of the laboratory.

Doc had his hat off now, since there was practically no chance of getting his head wet unless a pipe broke. He was busy removing the starfish from the wet sacks and arranging them on the cool concrete floor. The starfish were twisted and knotted up, for a starfish loves to hang on to something and for an hour these had found only each other. Doc arranged them in long lines and very slowly they straightened out until they lay in symmetrical stars on the concrete floor.

Doc's pointed brown beard was damp with perspiration as he worked. He looked up a little nervously as Mack entered. It was not that trouble always came in with Mack, but something always entered with him.

'Hiya, Doc?' said Mack.

'All right,' said Doc uneasily.

'Hear about Phyllis Mae over at the Bear Flag? She hit a drunk and got his tooth in her fist and it's infected clear to the elbow. She showed me the tooth. It was out of a plate. Is a false-tooth poison, Doc?'

'I guess everything that comes out the human mouth is poison,' said Doc warningfully. 'Has she got a doctor?'

'The bouncer fixed her up,' said Mack.

'I'll take her some sulfa,' said Doc, and he waited for the storm to break. He knew Mack had come for something and Mack knew he knew it.

Mack said: 'Doc, you got any need for any kind of animals now?'

Doc sighed with relief. 'Why?' he asked guardedly.

Mack became open and confidential. 'I'll tell you, Doc. I and the boys got to get some dough – we simply got to. It's for a good purpose, you might say a worthy cause.'

'Phyllis Mae's arm?'

Mack saw the chance, weighed it, and gave it up. 'Well – no,' he said. 'It's more important than that. You can't kill a whore. No – this is different. I and the boys thought if you needed something why we'd get it for you and that way we could make a little piece of change.'

It seemed simple and innocent. Doc laid down four more starfish in lines. 'I could use three or four hundred frogs,' he said. 'I'd get them myself, but I've got to go down to La Jolla tonight. There's a good tide tomorrow and I have to get some octopi.'

'Same price for frogs?' Mack asked. 'Five cents apiece.'

'Same price,' said Doc.

Mack was jovial. 'Don't you worry about frogs, Doc,' he said. 'We'll get you all the frogs you want. You just rest easy about frogs. Why we can get them right up Carmel River. I know a place.'

'Good,' said Doc. 'I'll take all you get, but I need about three hundred.'

'Just you rest easy, Doc. Don't you lose no sleep about it. You'll get your frogs, maybe seven eight hundred.' He put the Doc at his ease about frogs and then a little cloud crossed Mack's face. 'Doc,' he said, 'any chance of using your car to go up the Valley?'

'No,' said Doc. 'I told you. I have to drive to La Jolla tonight to make tomorrow's tide.'

'Oh,' said Mack dispiritedly. 'Oh. Well, don't you worry about it, Doc. Maybe we can get Lee Chong's old truck.' And then his face fell a little further. 'Doc,' he said, 'on a business deal like this, would you advance two or three bucks for petrol? I know Lee Chong won't give us petrol.'

'No,' said Doc. He had fallen into this before. Once he had financed Gay to go for turtles. He financed him for two weeks and at the end of that time Gay was in jail on his wife's charge and he never did go for turtles.

'Well, maybe we can't go then,' said Mack sadly.

Now Doc really needed the frogs. He tried to work out some method which was business and not philanthropy. 'I'll tell you what I'll do,' he said. 'I'll give you a note to my petrol station so you can get ten gallons of petrol. How will that be?'

Mack smiled. 'Fine,' he said. 'That will work out just fine. I and the boys will get an early start tomorrow. Time you get back from the south, we'll have more damn frogs than you ever seen in your life.'

Doc went to the labelling desk and wrote a note to Red Williams at the petrol station, authorizing the issue of ten gallons of petrol to Mack. 'Here you are,' he said.

Mack was smiling broadly. 'Doc,' he said, 'you can get to

sleep tonight and not even give frogs a thought. We'll have piss-pots full of them by the time you get back.'

Doc watched him go a little uneasily. Doc's dealings with Mack and the boys had always been interesting, but rarely had they been profitable to Doc. He remembered ruefully the time Mack sold him fifteen tom-cats and by night the owners came and got every one. 'Mack,' he had asked, 'why all tom-cats?'

Mack said: 'Doc, it's my own invention, but I'll tell you because you're a good friend. You make a big wire trap and then you don't use bait. You use – well – you use a lady cat. Catch every God-damn tom-cat in the country that way.'

From the laboratory Mack crossed the street and went through the swinging screen doors into Lee Chong's grocery. Mrs Lee was cutting bacon on the big butcher's block. A Lee cousin primped up slightly wilted heads of lettuce the way a girl primps a loose finger wave. A cat lay asleep on a big pile of oranges. Lee Chong stood in his usual place behind the cigar counter and in front of the liquor shelves. His tapping finger on the change mat speeded up a little when Mack came in.

Mack wasted no time in sparring. 'Lee,' he said, 'Doc over there's got a problem. He's got a big order for frogs from the New York Museum. Means a lot to Doc. Besides the dough there's a lot of credit getting an order like that. Doc's got to go south and I and the boys said we'd help him out. I think a guy's friends ought to help him out of a hole when they can, especially a nice guy like Doc. Why I bet he spends sixty seventy dollars a month with you.'

Lee Chong remained silent and watchful. His fat finger barely moved on the change mat, but it flicked slightly like a tense cat's tail.

Mack plunged into his thesis. 'Will you let us take your old truck to go up Carmel Valley for frogs for Doc – for good old Doc?'

Lee Chong smiled in triumph. 'Tluck no good,' he said. 'Bloke down.'

This staggered Mack for a moment, but he recovered. He spread the order for petrol on the cigar counter. 'Look!' he said 'Doc needs them frogs. He give me this order for petrol to get them. I can't let Doc down. Now Gay is a good mechanic. If he fixes your truck and puts it in good shape, will you let us take it?'

Lee put back his head so that he could see Mack through his half-glasses. There didn't seem to be anything wrong with the proposition. The truck really wouldn't run. Gay really was a good mechanic and the order for petrol was definite evidence of good faith.

'How long you be gone?' Lee asked.

'Maybe half a day, maybe a whole day. Just 'til we get the frogs.'

Lee was worried, but he couldn't see any way out. The dangers were all there and Lee knew all of them. 'Okay,' said Lee.

'Good,' said Mack. 'I knew Doc could depend on you. I'll get Gay right to work on that truck.' He turned about to leave. 'By the way,' he said. 'Doc's paying us five cents apiece for those frogs. We're going to get seven or eight hundred. How about taking a pint of Old Tennis Shoes just 'til we can get back with the frogs?'

'No!' said Lee Chong.

CHAPTER X

FRANKIE began coming to Western Biological when he was eleven years old. For a week or so he just stood outside the basement door and looked in. Then one day he stood inside the door. Ten days later he was in the basement. He had very large eyes and his hair was a dark wiry, dirty shock. His hands were filthy. He picked up a piece of excelsior and put it in a garbage can and then he looked at Doc where he worked labelling specimen bottles containing purple Velella. Finally Frankie got to the work-bench and he put his dirty fingers on the bench. It took Frankie three weeks to get that far, and he was ready to bolt every instant of the time.

Finally one day Doc spoke to him. 'What's your name, son?'

'Frankie.'

'Where do you live?'

'Up there,' a gesture up the hill.

'Why aren't you in school?'

'I don't go to school.'

'Why not?'

'They don't want me there.'

'Your hands are dirty. Don't you ever wash?'

Frankie looked stricken and then he went to the sink and scrubbed his hands, and always afterwards he scrubbed his hands almost raw every day.

And he came to the laboratory every day. It was an association without much talk. Doc by a telephone call established that what Frankie said was true. They didn't want him in school. He couldn't learn and there was something a little wrong with his co-ordination. There was no place for him. He wasn't an idiot, he wasn't dangerous, his parents, or parent, would not pay for his keep on an institution. Frankie didn't often sleep at the laboratory, but he spent his days there. And sometimes he crawled in the excelsior crate and slept. That was probably when there was a crisis at home.

Doc asked: 'Why do you come here?'

'You don't hit me or give me a nickel,' said Frankie.

'Do they hit you at home?'

'There's uncles around all the time at home. Some of them hit me and tell me to get out and some of them give me a nickel and tell me to get out.'

'Where's your father?'

'Dead,' said Frankie vaguely.

'Where's your mother?'

'With the uncles.'

Doc clipped Frankie's hair and got rid of the lice. At Lee Chong's he got him a new pair of overalls and a striped sweater and Frankie became his slave.

'I love you,' he said one afternoon. 'Oh, I love you.'

He wanted to work in the laboratory. He swept out every day, but there was something a little wrong. He couldn't get a floor quite clean. He tried to help with grading crayfish for size. There they were in a bucket, all sizes. They were to be grouped in the big pans – laid out – all the three-inch ones together and all the four-inch ones, and so forth. Frankie tried and the perspiration stood on his forehead, but he couldn't do it. Size relationships just didn't get through to him.

'No,' Doc would say. 'Look, Frankie. Put them beside your finger like this so you'll know which ones are this long. See? This one goes from the tip of your finger to the base of your thumb. Now you just pick out another one that goes from the tip of your finger down to the same place and it will be right.' Frankie tried and he couldn't do it. When

Doc went upstairs Frankie crawled in the excelsior box and didn't come out all afternoon.

But Frankie was a nice, good, kind boy. He learned to light Doc's cigars and wanted Doc to smoke all the time so he could light the cigars.

Better than anything else Frankie loved it when there were parties upstairs in the laboratory. When girls and men gathered to sit and talk, when the great phonograph played music that throbbed in his stomach and made beautiful and huge pictures form vaguely in his head. Frankie loved it. Then he crouched down in a corner behind a chair where he was hidden and could watch and listen. When there was laughter at a joke he didn't understand Frankie laughed delightedly behind his chair, and when the conversation dealt with abstractions his brow furrowed and he became intent and serious.

One afternoon he did a desperate thing. There was a small party in the laboratory. Doc was in the kitchen pouring beer when Frankie appeared beside him. Frankie grabbed a glass of beer and rushed it through the door and gave it to a girl sitting in a big chair.

She took the glass and said: 'Why, thank you,' and she smiled at him.

And Doc coming through the doors aid: 'Yes, Frankie is a great help to me.'

Frankie couldn't forget that. He did the thing in his mind over and over, just how he had taken the glass and just how the girl sat and then her voice – 'Why, thank you,' and Doc '– a great help to me – Frankie is a great help to me – sure Frankie is a great help – Frankie,' and Oh, my God!

He knew a big party was coming because Doc bought steaks and a great deal of beer and Doc let him help clean out all the upstairs. But that was nothing, for a great plan had formed in Frankie's mind and he could see just how it would be. He went over it again and again. It was beautiful. It was perfect.

Then the party started and people came and sat in the front room, girls and young women and men.

Frankie had to wait until he had the kitchen to himself, and the door closed. And it was some time before he had it so. But at last he was alone and the door was shut. He could hear the chatter of conversation and the music from the great phonograph. He worked very quietly – first the tray – then get out the glasses without breaking any. Now fill them with beer and let the foam settle a little and then fill again.

Now he was ready. He took a great breath and opened the door. The music and the talk roared around him. Frankie picked up the tray of beer and walked through the door. He knew how. He went straight toward the same young woman who had thanked him before. And then right in front of her, the thing happened, and co-ordination failed, the hands fumbled, the muscles panicked, the nerves telegraphed to a dead operator, the responses did not come back. Tray and beer collapsed forward into the young woman's lap. For a moment Frankie stood still. And then he turned and ran.

The room was quiet. They could hear him run downstairs and go into the cellar. They heard a hollow scrabbling sound – and then silence.

Doc walked quietly down the stairs and into the cellar. Frankie was in the excelsior box burrowed down clear to the bottom, with the pile of excelsior on top of him. Doc could hear him whimpering there. Doc waited for a moment and then he went quietly back upstairs.

There wasn't a thing in the world he could do.

CHAPTER XI

THE Model T Ford truck of Lee Chong had a dignified history. In 1923 it had been a passenger car belonging to Dr W. T. Waters. He used it for five years and sold it to an insurance man named Rattle. Mr Rattle was not a careful man. The car he got in clean nice condition he drove like fury. Mr Rattle drank on Saturday nights and the car suffered. The fenders were broken and bent. He was a pedal rider too and the bands had to be changed often. When Mr Rattle embezzled a client's money and ran away to San Jose, he was caught with a high-hair blonde and sent up within ten days.

The body of the car was so battered that its next owner cut it in two and added a little truck bed.

The next owner took off the front of the cab and the windshield. He used it to haul squids and he liked a fresh breeze to blow in his face. His name was Francis Almones, and he had a sad life, for he always made just a fraction less than he needed to live. His father had left him a little money, but year by year and month by month, no matter how hard Francis worked or how careful he was, his money grew less until he just dried up and blew away.

Lee Chong got the truck in payment of a grocery bill.

By this time the truck was little more than four wheels and an engine, and the engine was so crotchety and sullen and senile that it required expert care and consideration. Lee Chong did not give it these things, with the result that the truck stood in the tall grass back of the grocery most of the time with the mallows growing between its spokes. It had solid tyres on its back wheels and blocks held its front wheels off the ground.

Probably any one of the boys from the Palace Flophouse could have made the truck run, for they were all competent practical mechanics, but Gay was an inspired mechanic. There is no term comparable to green thumbs to apply to such a mechanic, but there should be. For there are men who can look, listen, tap, make an adjustment, and a machine works. Indeed there are men near whom a car runs better. And such a one was Gay. His fingers on a timer or a carburettor adjustment screw were gentle and wise and sure. He could fix the delicate electric motors in the laboratory. He could have worked in the canneries all the time had he wished, for in that industry, which complains bitterly when it does not make back its total investment every year in profits, the machinery is much less important than the fiscal statement. Indeed, if you could can sardines with ledgers, the owners would have been very happy. As it was they used decrepit, struggling old horrors of machines that needed the constant attention of a man like Gay.

Mack got the boys up early. They had their coffee and immediately moved over to the truck where it lay among the weeds. Gay was in charge. He kicked the blocked-up front wheels. 'Go borrow a pump and get those pumped up,' he said. Then he put a stick in the petrol-tank under the board which served as a seat. By some miracle there was a half-inch of petrol in the tank. Now Gay went over the most probable difficulties. He took out the coil boxes, scraped the points, adjusted the gap, and put them back. He opened the carburettor to see that petrol came through. He pushed on the crank to see that the whole shaft wasn't frozen and the pistons rusted in their cylinders.

Meanwhile the pump arrived and Eddie and Jones spelled each other on the tyres.

Gay hummed: 'Dum tiddy – dum tiddy,' as he worked. He removed the spark-plugs and scraped the points and

bored the carbon out. Then Gay drained a little petrol into
a can and poured some into each cylinder before he put the
spark-plugs back. He straightened up. 'We're going to need
a couple of dry cells,' he said. 'See if Lee Chong will let us
have a couple.'

Mack departed and returned almost immediately with a
universal No which was designed by Lee Chong to cover all
future requests.

Gay thought deeply. 'I know where's a couple – pretty
good ones too, but I won't go get them.'

'Where?' asked Mack.

'Down cellar at my house,' said Gay. 'They run the front-
door bell. If one of you fellas wants to kind of edge into my
cellar without my wife seeing you, they're on top of the
side stringer on the left-hand side as you go in. But for God's
sake, don't let my wife catch you.'

A conference elected Eddie to go and he departed.

'If you get caught don't mention me,' Gay called out after
him. Meanwhile Gay tested the bands. The low-high pedal
didn't quite touch the floor, so he knew there was a little
band left. The brake pedal did touch the floor, so there was
no brake, but the reverse pedal had lots of band left. On a
Model T Ford the reverse is your margin of safety. When
your brake is gone, you can use reverse as a brake. And when
the low gear band is worn too thin to pull up a steep hill,
why, you can turn round and back up it. Gay found there
was plenty of reverse and he knew everything was all right.

It was a good omen that Eddie came back with the dry
cells without trouble. Mrs Gay had been in the kitchen.
Eddie could hear her walking about, but she didn't hear
Eddie. He was very good at such things.

Gay connected the dry cells and he advanced the petrol
and retarded the spark-lever. 'Twist her tail,' he said.

He was such a wonder, Gay was – the little mechanic of
God, the St Francis of all things that turn and twist and
explode, the St Francis of coils and armatures and gears.

And if at some time all the heaps of cars, cut-down Dusenbergs, Buicks, De Sotos and Plymouths, American Austins and Isotta-Fraschinis praise God in a great chorus – it will be largely due to Gay and his brotherhood.

One twist – one little twist and the engine caught and laboured and faltered and caught again. Gay advanced the spark and reduced the petrol. He switched over to the magneto and the Ford of Lee Chong chuckled and jiggled and clattered happily as though it knew it was working for a man who loved and understood it.

There were two small technical legal difficulties with the truck – it had no recent licence plates and it had no lights. But the boys hung a rag permanently and accidentally on the rear plate to conceal its vintage and they dabbed the front plate with good thick mud. The equipment of the expedition was slight: some long-handled frog-nets and some gunny-sacks. City hunters going out for sport load themselves with food and liquor, but not Mack. He presumed rightly that the country was where food came from. Two loaves of bread and what was left of Eddie's wining jug was all the supply. The party clambered on the truck. Gay drove and Mack sat beside him; they bumped round the corner of Lee Chong's and down through the lot, threading among the pipes. Mr Malloy waved at them from his seat by the boiler. Gay eased across the pavement and down off the kerb gently because the front tyres showed fabric all the way around. With all their alacrity, it was afternoon when they got started.

The truck eased into Red Williams' service station. Mack got out and gave his paper to Red. He said: 'Doc was a little short of change. So if you'll put five gallons in and just give us a buck instead of the other five gallons, why, that's what Doc wants. He had to go south, you know. Had a big deal down there.'

Red smiled good-naturedly. 'You know, Mack,' he said, 'Doc got to figuring if there was some kind of loop-hole, and

he put his finger on the same one you did. Doc's a pretty
bright fellow. So he phoned me last night.'

'Put in the whole ten gallons,' said Mack. 'No – wait. It'll
slop around and spill. Put in five and give us five in a can –
one of them sealed cans.'

Red smiled happily. 'Doc kind of figured that one too,' he
said.

'Put in ten gallons,' said Mack. 'And don't go leaving
none in the hose.'

The little expedition did not go through the centre of
Monterey. A delicacy about the licence plates and the lights
made Gay choose back streets. There would be the time
when they would go up Carmel Hill and down into the Valley, a good four miles on a main highway, exposed to any
passing cop until they turned up the fairly unfrequented
Carmel Valley road. Gay chose a back street that brought
them out on the main highway at Peter's Gate just before
the steep Carmel Hill starts. Gay took a good noisy clatter-
ing run at the hill and in fifty yards he put the pedal down
too low. He knew it wouldn't work, the band was worn too
thin. On the level it was all right, but not on a hill. He
stopped, let the truck back round and aimed it down the hill.
Then he gave it the petrol and the reverse pedal. And the
reverse was not worn. The truck crawled steadily and slowly
but backward up Carmel Hill.

And they very nearly made it. The radiator boiled, of
course, but most Model T experts believed that it wasn't
working well if it wasn't boiling.

Someone should write an erudite essay on the moral,
physical, and aesthetic effect of the Model T Ford on the
American nation. Two generations of Americans knew more
about the Ford coil than the clitoris, about the planetary
system of gears than the solar system of stars. With the Model
T, part of the concept of private property disappeared. Pliers
ceased to be privately owned and a tyre-pump belonged to
the last man who had picked it up. Most of the babies of the

period were conceived in Model T Fords and not a few were born in them. The theory of the Anglo-Saxon home became so warped that it never quite recovered.

The truck backed sturdily up Carmel Hill and it got past the Jack's Peak road and was just going into the last and steepest pull when the motor's breathing thickened, gulped, and strangled. It seemed very quiet when the motor was still. Gay, who was heading down-hill, anyway, ran down the hill fifty feet and turned into the Jack's Peak road entrance.

'What is it?' Mack asked.

'Carburettor, I think,' said Gay. The engine sizzled and creaked with heat and the jet of steam that blew down the overflow-pipe sounded like the hiss of an alligator.

The carburettor of a Model T is not complicated, but it needs all of its parts to function. There is a needle valve, and the point must be on the needle and must sit in its hole or the carburettor does not work.

Gay held the needle in his hand and the point was broken off. 'How in the hell you s'pose that happened?' he asked.

'Magic,' said Mack, 'just pure magic. Can you fix it?'

'Hell, no,' said Gay. 'Got to get another one.'

'How much they cost?'

'About a buck if you buy one new – quarter at a wrecker's.'

'You got a buck?' Mack asked.

'Yeah, but I won't need it.'

'Well, get back as soon as you can, will you? We'll just stay right here.'

'Anyways, you won't go running off without a needle valve,' said Gay. He stepped out to the road. He thumbed three cars before one stopped for him. The boys watched him climb in and start down the hill. They didn't see him again for one hundred and eighty days.

Oh, the infinity of possibility! How could it happen that the car that picked up Gay broke down before it got into Monterey? If Gay had not been a mechanic, he would not have fixed the car. If he had not fixed it the owner wouldn't have taken him to Jimmy Brucia's for a drink. And why was it Jimmy's birthday? Out of all the possibilities in the world – the millions of them – only events occurred that lead to the Salinas jail. Sparky Enea and Tiny Colletti had made up a quarrel and were helping Jimmy to celebrate his birthday. The blonde came in. The musical argument in front of the juke-box. Gay's new friend who knew a judo hold and tried to show it to Sparky and got his wrist broken when the hold went wrong. The policeman with a bad stomach – all unrelated, irrelevant details and yet all running in one direction. Fate just didn't intend Gay to go on that frog-hunt, and Fate took a hell of a lot of trouble and people and accidents to keep him from it. When the final climax came with the front of Holman's bootery broken out and the party trying on the shoes in the display window only Gay didn't hear the fire whistle. Only Gay didn't go to the fire, and when the police came they found him sitting all alone in Holman's window wearing one brown Oxford and one patent leather dress shoe with a grey cloth top.

Back at the truck the boys built a little fire when it got dark and the chill crept up from the ocean. The pines above them soughed in the fresh sea wind. The boys lay in the pine-needles and looked at the lonely sky through the pine branches. For a while they spoke of the difficulties Gay must be having getting a needle valve, and then gradually as the time passed they didn't mention him any more.

'Somebody should of gone with him,' said Mack.

About ten o'clock Eddie got up. 'There's a construction camp a piece up the hill,' he said. 'I think I'll go up and see if they got any Model T's.'

CHAPTER XII

MONTEREY is a city with a long and brilliant literary tradition. It remembers with pleasure and some glory that Robert Louis Stevenson lived there. Treasure Island certainly has the topography and the coastal plan of Pt Lobos. More recently in Carmel there have been a great number of literary men about, but there is not the old flavour, the old dignity of the true *belles-lettres*. Once the town was greatly outraged over what the citizens considered a slight to an author. It had to do with the death of Josh Billings, the great humorist.

Where the new post office is, there used to be a deep gulch with water flowing in it and a little foot-bridge over it. On one side of the gulch was a fine old adobe and on the other the house of the doctor who handled all the sickness, birth, and death in the town. He worked with animals too and, having studied in France, he even dabbled in the new practice of embalming bodies before they were buried. Some of the old-timers considered this sentimental and some thought it wasteful, and to some it was sacrilegious since there was no provision for it in any sacred volume. But the better and richer families were coming to it, and it looked to become a fad.

One morning elderly Mr Carriaga was walking from his house on the hill down toward Alvarado Street. He was just crossing the foot-bridge when his attention was drawn to a small boy and a dog struggling up out of the gulch. The boy carried a liver while the dog dragged yards of intestine at the end of which a stomach dangled. Mr Carriaga paused and addressed the little boy politely: 'Good morning.'

In those days little boys were courteous. 'Good morning, sir.'

'Where are you going with the liver?'

'I'm going to make some chum and catch some mackerel.'

Mr Carriaga smiled. 'And the dog, will he catch mackerel too?'

'The dog found that. It's his, sir. We found them in the gulch.'

Mr Carriaga smiled and strolled on and then his mind began to work. That isn't a beef liver, it's too small. And it isn't a calf's liver, it's too red. It isn't a sheep's liver ... Now his mind was alert. At the corner he met Mr Ryan.

'Anyone die in Monterey last night?' he asked.

'Not that I know of,' said Mr Ryan.

'Anyone killed?'

'No.'

They walked on together and Mr Carriaga told about the little boy and the dog.

At the 'Adobe Bar' a number of citizens were gathered for their morning conversation. There Mr Carriaga told his story again, and he had just finished when the constable came into the 'Adobe'. He should know if anyone had died. 'No one died in Monterey,' he said. 'But Josh Billings died out at the Hotel del Monte.'

The men in the bar were silent. And the same thought went through all their minds. Josh Billings was a great man, a great writer. He had honoured Monterey by dying there and he had been degraded. Without much discussion a committee formed made up of everyone there. The stern men walked quickly to the gulch and across the foot-bridge and they hammered on the door of the doctor who had studied in France.

He had worked late. The knocking got him out of bed and brought him tousled of hair and beard to the door in his nightgown. Mr Carriaga addressed him sternly: 'Did you embalm Josh Billings?'

'Why – yes.'

'What did you do with his "inards"?'

'Why – I threw them in the gulch where I always do.'

They made him dress quickly then and they hurried down to the beach. If the little boy had gone quickly about his business, it would have been too late. He was just getting into a boat when the committee arrived. The intestine was in the sand where the dog had abandoned it.

Then the French doctor was made to collect the parts. He was forced to wash them reverently and pick out as much sand as possible. The doctor himself had to stand the expense of the leaden box which went into the coffin of Josh Billings. For Monterey was not a town to let dishonour come to a literary man.

CHAPTER XIII

MACK and the boys slept peacefully on the pine-needles. Some time before dawn Eddie came back. He had gone a long way before he found a Model T. And then when he did, he wondered whether or not it would be a good idea to take the needle out of its seat. It might not fit. So he took the whole carburettor. The boys didn't wake up when he got back. He lay down beside them and slept under the pine-trees. There was one nice thing about Model T's. The parts were not only interchangeable, they were unidentifiable.

There is a beautiful view from the Carmel grade, the curving bay with the waves creaming on the sand, the dune country around Seaside and right at the bottom of the hill, the warm intimacy of the town.

Mack got up in the dawn and hustled his pants where they bound him and he stood looking down on the bay. He could see some of the purse-seiners coming in. A tanker stood over against Seaside, taking on oil. Behind him the rabbits stirred in the bush. Then the sun came up and shook the night chill out of the air the way you'd shake a rug. When he felt the first sun warmth, Mack shivered.

The boys ate a little bread while Eddie installed the new carburettor. And when it was ready, they didn't bother to crank it. They pushed it out to the highway and coasted in gear until it started. And then, Eddie driving, they backed up over the rise, over the top and turned and headed forward and down past Hatton Fields. In Carmel Valley the artichoke plants stood grey-green, and the willows were lush along the river. They turned left up the valley. Luck blossomed from the first. A dusty Rhode Island red rooster who had wandered too far from his own farmyard crossed the road and Eddie hit him without running too far off the road. Sitting in the back of the truck, Hazel picked him as they went and let the feathers fly from his hand, the most widely distributed evidence on record, for there was a little breeze in the morning blowing down from Jamesburg and some of the red chicken feathers were deposited on Pt Lobos and some even blew out to sea.

The Carmel is a lovely little river. It isn't very long, but in its course it has everything a river should have. It rises in the mountains, and tumbles down a while, runs through shallows, is dammed to make a lake, spills over the dam, crackles among round boulders, wanders lazily under sycamores, spills into pools where trout live, drops in against banks where crayfish live. In the winter it becomes a torrent, a mean little fierce river, and in the summer it is a place for children to wade in and for fishermen to wander in. Frogs blink from its banks and the deep ferns grow beside it. Deer and foxes come to drink from it, secretly in the morning and evening, and now and then a mountain lion crouched flat laps its water. The farms of the rich little valley back up to the river and take its water for the orchards and the vegetables. The quail call beside it and the wild doves come whistling in at dusk. Raccoons pace its edges looking for frogs. It's everything a river should be.

A few miles up the valley the river cuts in under a high cliff from which vines and ferns hang down. At the base of this cliff there is a pool, green and deep, and on the other side of the pool there is a little sandy place where it is good to sit and to cook your dinner.

Mack and the boys came down to this place happily. It was perfect. If frogs were available, they would be here. It was a place to relax, a place to be happy. On the way out they had thriven. In addition to the big red chicken there was a sack of carrots which had fallen from a vegetable truck, half a dozen onions which had not. Mack had a bag of coffee in his pocket. In the truck there was a five-gallon can with the top cut off. The wining-jug was nearly half full. Such things as salt and pepper had been brought. Mack and the boys would have thought anyone who travelled without salt, pepper, and coffee very silly indeed.

Without effort, confusion, or much thought, four round stones were rolled together on the little beach. The rooster who had challenged the sunrise of this very day lay dismembered and clean in water in the five-gallon can with peeled onions about him, while a little fire of dead willow sticks sputtered between the stones, a very little fire. Only fools build big fires. It would take a long time to cook this rooster, for it had taken him a long time to achieve this size and muscularity. But as the water began to boil gently about him, he smelled good from the beginning.

Mack gave them a pep talk. 'The best time for frogs is at night,' he said, 'so I guess we'll just lay around 'til it gets dark.' They sat in the shade and gradually one by one they stretched out and slept.

Mack was right. Frogs do not move around much in the

day-time; they hide under ferns and they look secretly out of holes under rocks. The way to catch frogs is with a flash-light at night. The men slept knowing they might have a very active night. Only Hazel stayed awake to replenish the little fire under the cooking chicken.

There is no golden afternoon next to the cliff. When the sun went over it at about two o'clock a whispering shade came to the beach. The sycamores rustled in the afternoon breeze. Little water-snakes slipped down to the rocks and then gently entered the water and swam along through the pool, their heads held up like little periscopes and a tiny wake spreading behind them. A big trout jumped in the pool. The gnats and mosquitoes which avoid the sun came out and buzzed over the water. All of the sun bugs, the flies, the dragonflies, the wasps, the hornets, went home. And as the shadow came to the beach, as the first quail began to call, Mack and the boys awakened. The smell of the chicken stew was heart-breaking. Hazel had picked a fresh bay-leaf from a tree by the river and he had dropped it in. The carrots were in now. Coffee in its own can was simmering on its own rock, far enough from the flame so that it did not boil too hard. Mack awakened, started up, stretched, stag-gered to the pool, washed his face with cupped hands, hacked, spat, washed out his mouth, broke wind, tightened his belt, scratched his legs, combed his wet hair with his fingers, drank from the jug, belched, and sat down by the fire. 'By God that smells good,' he said.

Men all do about the same things when they wake up. Mack's process was loosely the one all of them followed. And soon they had all come to the fire and complimented Hazel. Hazel stuck his pocket-knife into the muscles of the chicken.

'He ain't going to be what you'd call tender,' said Hazel. 'You'd have to cook him about two weeks to get him tender. How old about do you judge he was, Mack?'

'I'm forty-eight and I ain't as tough as he is,' said Mack. Eddie said: 'How old can a chicken get, do you think –

that's if nobody pushed him around or he don't get sick?'

'That's something nobody isn't ever going to find out,' said Jones.

It was a pleasant time. The jug went around and warmed them.

Jones said: 'Eddie, I don't mean to complain none. I was just thinkin'. S'pose you had two or three jugs back of the bar. S'pose you put all the whisky in one and all the wine in another and all the beer in another . . .'

A slightly shocked silence followed the suggestion. 'I didn't mean nothing,' said Jones quickly. 'I like it this way . . .' Jones talked too much then because he knew he had made a social blunder and he wasn't able to stop. 'What I like about it this way is you never know what kind of a drunk you're going to get out of it,' he said. 'You take whisky,' he said hurriedly. 'You more or less know what you'll do. A fightin' guy fights and a cryin' guy cries, but this' – he said magnanimously – 'why, you don't know whether it'll run you up a pine-tree or start you swimming to Santa Cruz. It's more fun that way,' he said weakly.

'Speaking of swimming,' said Mack to fill in the indelicate place in the conversation and to shut Jones up. 'I wonder whatever happened to that guy McKinley Moran. Remember that deep-sea diver?'

'I remember him,' said Hughie. 'I and him used to hang around together. He just didn't get much work and then he got to drinking. It's kind of tough on you divin' and drinkin'. Got to worryin' too. Finally he sold his suit and helmet and pump and went on a hell of a drunk and then he left town. I don't know where he went. He wasn't no good after he went down after that Wop that got took down with the anchor from the *Twelve Brothers*. McKinley just dove down. Bust his ear-drums, and he wasn't no good after that. Didn't hurt the Wop a bit.'

Mack sampled the jug again. 'He used to make a lot of

dough during Prohibition,' Mack said. 'Used to get twenty-five bucks a day from the government to dive lookin' for liquor on the bottom and he got three dollars a case from Louie for not findin' it. Had it worked out so he brought up one case a day to keep the government happy. Louie didn't mind that none. Made it so they didn't get in no new divers. McKinley made a lot of dough.'

'Yeah,' said Hughie. 'But he's like everybody else – gets some dough and he wants to get married. He got married three times before his dough run out. I could always tell. He'd buy a white fox piece and bang! – next thing you'd know, he's married.'

'I wonder what happened to Gay,' Eddie asked. It was the first time they had spoken of him.

'Same thing, I guess,' said Mack. 'You just can't trust a married guy. No matter how much he hates his old lady why he'll go back to her. Get to thinkin' and broodin' and back he'll go. You can't trust him no more. Take Gay,' said Mack. 'His old lady hits him. But I bet you when Gay's away from her three days, he gets it figured out that it's his fault and he goes back to make it up to her.'

They ate long and daintily, spearing out pieces of chicken, holding the dripping pieces until they cooled, and then gnawing the muscled meat from the bone. They speared the carrots on pointed willow switches and finally they passed the can and drank the juice. And around them the evening crept in as delicately as music. The quail called each other down to the water. The trout jumped in the pool. And the moths came down and fluttered about the pool as the daylight mixed into the darkness. They passed the coffee-can about and they were warm and fed and silent. At last Mack said: 'God damn it. I hate a liar.'

'Who's been lyin' to you?' Eddie asked.

'Oh, I don't mind a guy that tells a little one to get along or to hop up a conversation, but I hate a guy that lies to himself.'

'Who done that?' Eddie asked.

'Me,' said Mack. 'And maybe you guys. Here we are,' he said 'earnestly, the whole God damned shabby lot of us. We worked it out that we wanted to give Doc a party. So we come out here and have a hell of a lot of fun. Then we'll go back and get the dough from Doc. There's five of us, so we'll drink five times as much liquor as he will. And I ain't sure we're doin' it for Doc. I ain't sure we ain't doin' it for ourselves. And Doc's too nice a fella to do that to. Doc is the nicest fella I ever knew. I don't want to be the kind of a guy that would take advantage of him. You know one time I put the bee on him for a buck. I give him a hell of a story. Right in the middle I seen he knew God damn well the story was so much malarky. So right in the middle I says: "Doc, that's a fuggin' lie!" And he put his hand in his pocket and brought out a buck. "Mack," he says, "I figure a guy that needs it bad enough to make up a lie to get it, really needs it," and he give me the buck. I paid him that buck back the next day. I never did spend it. Just kept it overnight and then give it back to him.'

Hazel said: 'There ain't nobody likes a party better than Doc. We're givin' him the party. What the hell is the beef?'

'I don't know,' said Mack, 'I'd like just to give him something when I didn't get most of it back.'

'How about a present?' Hughie suggested. 'S'pose we just bought the whisky and give it to him and let him do what he wants.'

'Now you're talkin',' said Mack. 'That's just what we'll do. We'll just give him the whisky and fade out.'

'You know what'll happen,' said Eddie. 'Henri and them people from Carmel will smell that whisky out and then instead of only five of us there'll be twenty. Doc told me one time himself they can smell him fryin' a steak from Cannery Row clear down to Point Sur. I don't see the percentage. He'd come out better if we give him the party ourselves.'

Mack considered this reasoning. 'Maybe you're right,' he

said at last. 'But s'pose we give him something except whisky, maybe cuff-links with his initials.'

'Oh, horse shit,' said Hazel. 'Doc don't want stuff like that.'

The night was in by now and the stars were white in the sky. Hazel fed the fire and it put a little room of light on the beach. Over the hill a fox was barking sharply. And now in the night the smell of sage came down from the hills. The water chuckled on the stones where it went out of the deep pool.

Mack was mulling over the last piece of reasoning when the sound of footsteps on the ground made them turn. A man dark and large stalked near and he had a shot-gun over his arm and a pointer walked shyly and delicately at his heel.

'What the hell are you doing here?' he asked.

'Nothing,' said Mack.

'The land's posted. No fishing, hunting, fires, camping. Now you just pack up and put that fire out and get off this land.'

Mack stood up humbly. 'I didn't know, Captain,' he said. 'Honest we never seen the sign, Captain.'

'There's signs all over. You couldn't have missed them.'

'Look, Captain, we made a mistake and we're sorry,' said Mack. He paused and looked closely at the slouching figure. 'You are a military man, aren't you, sir? I can always tell. Military man don't carry his shoulders the same as ordinary people. I was in the army so long, I can always tell.'

Imperceptibly the shoulders of the man straightened, nothing obvious, but he held himself differently.

'I don't allow fires on my place,' he said.

'Well, we're sorry,' said Mack. 'We'll get right out, Captain. You see, we're workin' for some scientist. We're goin' to get some frogs. They're working on cancer and we're helpin' out getting some frogs.'

The man hesitated for a moment. 'What do they do with the frogs?' he asked.

'Well, sir,' said Mack, 'they give cancer to the frogs and then they can study and experiment and they got it nearly licked if they can just get some frogs. But if you don't want us on your land, Captain, we'll get right out. Never would of come in if we knew.' Suddenly Mack seemed to see the pointer for the first time. 'By God that's a fine-lookin' bitch,' he said enthusiastically. 'She looks like Nola that win the field trials in Virginia last year. She a Virginia dog, Captain?'

The captain hesitated and then he lied. 'Yes,' he said shortly. 'She's lame. Tick got her right on her shoulder.'

Mack was instantly solicitous. 'Mind if I look, Captain? Come, girl. Come on, girl.' The pointer looked up at her master and then sidled up to Mack. 'Pile on some twigs so I can see,' he said to Hazel.

'It's up where she can't lick it,' said the captain, and he leaned over Mack's shoulder to look.

Mack pressed some pus out of the evil-looking crater on the dog's shoulder. 'I had a dog once had a thing like this and it went right in and killed him. She just had pups, didn't she?'

'Yes,' said the captain, 'six. I put iodine on that place.'

'No,' said Mack, 'that won't draw. You got any Epsom salts up at your place?'

'Yes – there's a big bottle.'

'Well, you make a hot poultice of Epsom salts and put it on there. She's weak, you know, from the pups. Be a shame if she got sick now. You'd lose the pups too.' The pointer looked deep into Mack's eyes and then she licked his hand.

'Tell you what I'll do, Captain. I'll look after her myself. Epsom salt'll do the trick. That's the best thing.'

The captain stroked the dog's head. 'You know, I've got a pond up by the house that's so full of frogs I can't sleep nights. Why don't you look up there? They bellow all night. I'd be glad to get rid of them.'

'That's mighty nice of you,' said Mack. 'I'll bet those docs would thank you for that. But I'd like to get a poultice on this dog.' He turned to the others. 'You put out this fire,' he said. 'Make sure there ain't a spark left and clean up around. You don't want to leave no mess. I and the captain will go and take care of Nola here. You fellows follow along when you get cleared up.' Mack and the captain walked away together.

Hazel kicked sand on the fire. 'I bet Mack could of been president of the US if he wanted,' he said.

'What could he do with it if he had it?' Jones asked. 'There wouldn't be no fun in that.'

CHAPTER XIV

EARLY morning is a time of magic in Cannery Row. In the grey time after the light has come and before the sun has risen, the Row seems to hang suspended out of time in a silvery light. The street lights go out, and the weeds are a brilliant green. The corrugated iron of the canneries glows with the pearly lucence of platinum or old pewter. No auto-mobiles are running then. The street is silent of progress and business. And the rush and drag of the waves can be heard as they splash in among the piles of the canneries. It is a time of great peace, a deserted time, a little era of rest. Cats drip over the fences and slither like syrup over the ground to look for fish-heads. Silent early-morning dogs parade majestically, picking and choosing judiciously whereon to pee. The sea-gulls come flapping in to sit on the cannery roofs to await the day of refuse. They sit on the roof peaks shoulder to shoulder. From the rocks near the Hopkins Marine Station comes the barking of sea-lions like the baying of hounds. The air is cool and fresh. In the back gardens the gophers push up the morning mounds of fresh damp earth and they creep out and drag flowers into their holes. Very few people are about, just enough to make it seem more deserted than it is. One of Dora's girls comes home from a call on a patron too wealthy or too sick to visit the Bear Flag. Her make-up is a little sticky and her feet are tired. Lee Chong brings the garbage cans out and stands them on the kerb. The old Chinaman comes out of the sea and flap-flaps across the street and up past the Palace. The cannery watchmen look out and blink at the morning light. The bouncer at the Bear Flag steps out on the porch in his shirt-sleeves and stretches and yawns and scratches his stomach. The snores of Mr Malloy's tenants in the pipes have a deep tunnelly quality. It is the hour of the pearl – the interval between day and night when time stops and examines itself.

On such a morning and in such a light two soldiers and two girls strolled easily along the street. They had come out of 'La Ida' and they were very tired and very happy. The girls were hefty, big-breasted, and strong and their blonde hair was in slight disarray. They wore printed rayon party dresses, wrinkled now and clinging to their convexities. And each girl wore a soldier's cap, one far back on her head and the other with the visor down almost on her nose. They were full-lipped, broad-nosed, hippy girls and they were very tired.

The soldiers' tunics were unbuttoned and their belts were threaded through their epaulettes. The ties were pulled down a little so the shirt-collars could be unbuttoned. And the soldiers wore the girls' hats, one a tiny yellow straw boater with a bunch of daisies on the crown, the other a white knitted half-hat to which medallions of blue cellophane adhered. They walked holding hands, swinging their

hands rhythmically. The soldier on the outside had a large
brown paper bag filled with cold canned beer. They strolled
softly in the pearly light. They had had a hell of a time and
they felt good. They smiled delicately like weary children
remembering a party. They looked at one another and
smiled and they swung their hands. Past the Bear Flag they
went and said 'Hiya' to the bouncer who was scratching his
stomach. They listened to the snores from the pipes and
laughed a little. At Lee Chong's they stopped and looked
into the messy display window where tools and clothes and
food crowded for attention. Swinging their hands and scuf-
fing their feet, they came to the end of Cannery Row and
turned up to the railroad track. The girls climbed on the
rails and walked along on them and the soldiers put their
arms around the plump waists to keep them from falling.
Then they went past the boat-works and turned down into
the park-like property of the Hopkins Marine Station.
There is a tiny curved beach in front of the station, a minia-
ture beach between little reefs. The gentle morning waves
licked up the beach and whispered softly. The fine smell of
seaweed came from the exposed rocks. As the four came to
the beach a sliver of the sun broke over Tom Work's land
across the head of the bay and it gilded the water and made
the rocks yellow. The girls sat formally down in the sand and
straightened their skirts over their knees. One of the soldiers
punched holes in four cans of beer and handed them round.
And then the men lay down and put their heads in the girls'
laps and looked up into their faces. And they smiled at each
other, a tired and peaceful and wonderful secret.

From up near the station came the barking of a dog – the
watchman, a dark and surly man, had seen them and his
black and surly cocker spaniel had seen them. He shouted
at them, and when they did not move he came down on the
beach and his dog barked monotonously. 'Don't you know
you can't lay around here? You got to get off. This is private
property!'

The soldiers did not even seem to hear him. They smiled on and the girls were stroking their hair over the temples. At last in slow motion one of the soldiers turned his head so that his cheek was cradled between the girl's legs. He smiled benevolently at the caretaker. 'Why don't you take a flying fuggut the moon?' he said kindly, and he turned back to look at the girl.

The sun lighted her blonde hair and she scratched him over one ear. They didn't even see the caretaker go back to his house.

CHAPTER XV

By the time the boys got up to the farm-house Mack was in the kitchen. The pointer bitch lay on her side, and Mack held a cloth saturated with Epsom salts against her tick-bite. Among her legs the big fat wiener pups nuzzled and bumped for milk and the bitch looked patiently up into Mack's face, saying: 'You see how it is? I try to tell him, but he doesn't understand.'

The captain held a lamp and looked down on Mack.

'I'm glad to know about that,' he said.

Mack said: 'I don't want to tell you about your business, sir, but these pups ought to be weaned. She ain't got a hell of a lot of milk left and them pups are chewin' her to pieces.'

'I know,' said the captain. 'I s'pose I should have drowned them all but one. I've been so busy trying to keep the place going. People don't take the interest in bird dogs they used to. It's all poodles and boxers and Dobermans.'

'I know,' said Mack. 'And there ain't no dog like a pointer for a man. I don't know what's come over people. But you wouldn't of drowned them, would you, sir?'

'Well,' said the captain, 'since my wife went into politics, I'm just running crazy. She got elected to the Assembly for this district and when the Legislature isn't in session, she's off making speeches. And when she's home she's studying all the time and writing bills.'

'Must be lousy in – I mean it must be pretty lonely,' said Mack. 'Now if I had a pup like this' – he picked up a squirming puzz-faced pup – 'why, I bet I'd have a real bird dog in three years. I'd take a bitch every time.'

'Would you like to have one?' the captain asked.

Mack looked up. 'You mean you'd let me have one? Oh! Jesus Christ yes.'

'Take your pick,' said the Captain. 'Nobody seems to understand bird dogs any more.'

The boys stood in the kitchen and gathered quick impressions. It was obvious that the wife was away – the opened cans, the frying-pan with lace from fried egg still sticking to it, the crumbs on the kitchen table, the open box of shotgun shells on the bread-box all shrieked of the lack of a woman, while the white curtains and the papers on the dish shelves and the too small towels on the rack told them a woman had been there. And they were unconsciously glad she wasn't there. The kind of women who put papers on shelves and had little towels like that instinctively distrusted and disliked Mack and the boys. Such women knew that they were the worst threats to a home, for they offered ease and thought and companionship as opposed to neatness, order, and properness. They were glad she was away.

Now the captain seemed to feel that they were doing him a favour. He didn't want them to leave. He said hesitantly: 'S'pose you boys would like a little something to warm you up before you go out for the frogs?'

The others looked at Mack. Mack was frowning as though he was thinking it through. 'When we're out doin' scientific stuff, we make it a kind of a rule not to touch nothin',' he said, and then quickly, as though he might have gone too far: 'But seein' as how you been so nice to us – well, I wouldn't mind a short one myself. I don't know about the boys.'

The boys agreed that they wouldn't mind a short one either. The captain got a flashlight and went down in the cellar. They could hear him moving lumber and boxes about, and he came back upstairs with a five-gallon oak keg in his arms. He set it on the table. 'During Prohibition I got some corn whisky and laid it away. I just got to thinking I'd like to see how it is. It's pretty old now. I'd almost forgot it. You see – my wife . . .' he let it go at that because it was apparent that they understood. The captain knocked out the oak plug from the end of the keg and got glasses down from the shelf that had scallop-edged paper laid on it. It is a hard job to pour a small drink from a five-gallon keg. Each of them got half a water-glass of the clear brown liquor. They waited ceremoniously for the captain and then they said: 'Over the river,' and tossed it back. They swallowed, tasted their tongues, sucked their lips, and there was a far-away look in their eyes.

Mack peered into his empty glass as though some holy message was written in the bottom. And then he raised his eyes. 'You can't say nothin' about that,' he said. 'They don't put that in bottles.' He breathed in deeply and sucked his breath as it came out. 'I don't think I ever tasted nothin' as good as that,' he said.

The captain looked pleased. His glance wandered back to the keg. 'It is good,' he said. 'You think we might have another little one?'

Mack stared into his glass again. 'Maybe a short one,' he agreed. 'Wouldn't it be easier to pour out some in a pitcher? You're liable to spill it that way.'

Two hours later they recalled what they had come for.

The frog pool was square – fifty feet wide and seventy feet long and four feet deep. Lush soft grass grew about its edge and a little ditch brought the water from the river to it and

from it little ditches went out to the orchards. There were
frogs there all right, thousands of them. Their voices beat
the night, they boomed and barked and croaked and rattled.
They sang to the stars, to the waning moon, to the waving
grasses. They bellowed love songs and challenges. The men
crept through the darkness towards the pool. The captain
carried a nearly-filled pitcher of whisky and every man had
his own glass. The captain had found them flash-lights that
worked. Hughie and Jones carried gunny-sacks. As they
drew quietly near, the frogs heard them coming. The night
had been roaring with frog song and then suddenly it was
silent. Mack and the boys and the captain sat down on the
ground to have one last short one and to map their campaign. And the plan was bold.

During the millennia that frogs and men have lived in the
same world, it is probable that men have hunted frogs. And
during that time a pattern of hunt and parry has developed.
The man with net or bow or lance or gun creeps noiselessly,
as he thinks, toward the frog. The pattern requires that the
frog sit still, sit very still and wait. The rules of the game
require the frog to wait until the final flicker of a second,
when the net is descending, when the lance is in the air,
when the finger squeezes the trigger, then the frog jumps,
plops into the water, swims to the bottom, and waits until
the man goes away. That is the way it is done, the way it
has always been done. Frogs have every right to expect it
will always be done that way. Now and then the net is too
quick, the lance pierces, the gun flicks, and that frog is gone,
but it is all fair and in the frame-work. Frogs don't resent
that. But how could they have anticipated Mack's new
method? How could they have foreseen the horror that
followed? The sudden flashing of lights, the shouting and
squealing of men, the rush of feet. Every frog leaped, plopped
into the pool, and swam frantically to the bottom. Then
into the pool plunged the line of men, stamping, churning,
moving in a crazy line up the pool, flinging their feet about.

Hysterically the frogs, displaced from their placid spots, swam ahead of the crazy thrashing feet and the feet came on. Frogs are good swimmers, but they haven't much endurance. Down the pool they went until finally they were bunched and crowded against the ends. And the feet and wildly-plunging bodies followed them. A few frogs lost their heads and floundered among the feet and got through and these were saved. But the majority decided to leave this pool for ever, to find a new home in a new country where this kind of thing didn't happen. A wave of frantic, frustrated frogs, big ones, little ones, brown ones, green ones, men frogs and women frogs, a wave of them broke over the bank, crawled, leaped, scrambled. They clambered up the grass, they clutched at each other, little ones rode on big ones. And then – horror on horror – the flashlights found them. Two men gathered them like berries. The line came out of the water and closed in on their rear and gathered them like potatoes. Tens and fifties of them were flung into the gunny-sacks and the sacks filled with tired, frightened, and disillusioned frogs, with dripping, whimpering frogs. Some got away, of course, and some had been saved in the pool. But never in frog history had such an execution taken place. Frogs by the pound, by the fifty pounds. They weren't counted, but there must have been six or seven hundred. Then happily Mack tied up the necks of the sacks. They were soaking, dripping wet and the air was cool. They had a short one in the grass before they went back to the house, so they wouldn't catch cold.

It is doubtful whether the captain had ever had so much fun. He was indebted to Mack and the boys. Later when the curtains caught fire and were put out with the little towels, the captain told the boys not to mind it. He felt it was an honour to have them burn his house clear down, if they wanted to. 'My wife is a wonderful woman,' he said in a kind of peroration. 'Most wonderful woman. Ought to of been a man. If she was a man I wouldn' of married her.'

He laughed a long time over that and repeated it three or four times and resolved to remember it, so he could tell it to a lot of other people. He filled a jug with whisky and gave it to Mack. He wanted to go to live with them in the Palace Flophouse. He decided that his wife would like Mack and the boys if she only knew them. Finally, he went to sleep on the floor with his head among the puppies. Mack and the boys poured themselves a short one and regarded him seriously.

Mack said: 'He give me that jug of whisky, didn't he? You heard him?'

'Sure he did,' said Eddie. 'I heard him.'

'And he give me a pup?'

'Sure, pick of the litter. We all heard him. Why?'

'I never did roll a drunk and I ain't gonna start now,' said Mack. 'We got to get out of here. He's gonna wake up feelin' lousy and it's goin' to be all our fault. I just don't want to be here.' Mack glanced at the burned curtains, at the floor glistening with whisky and puppy dirt, at the bacon grease that was coagulating on the stove front. He went to the pups, looked them over carefully, felt bone and frame, looked in eyes, and regarded jaws, and he picked out a beautifully-spotted bitch with a liver-coloured nose and a fine dark-yellow eye. 'Come on, darling,' he said.

They blew out the lamp because of the danger of fire. It was just turning dawn as they left the house.

'I don't think I ever had such a fine trip,' said Mack. 'But I got to thinkin' about his wife comin' back and it gave me the shivers.' The pup whined in his arms and he put it under his coat. 'He's a real nice fella,' said Mack. 'After you get him feelin' easy, that is.' He strode on toward the place where they had parked the Ford. 'We shouldn't go forgettin' we're doin' all this for Doc,' he said. 'From the way things are pannin' out, it looks like Doc is a pretty lucky guy.'

CHAPTER XVI

PROBABLY the busiest time the girls of the Bear Flag ever had was the March of the big sardine catch. It wasn't only that the fish ran in silvery billions and money ran almost as freely. A new regiment moved into the Presidio and a new bunch of soldiers always shop around a good deal before they settle down. Dora was short-handed just at that time too, for Eva Flanagan had gone to East St Louis on a vacation, Phyllis Mae had broken her leg getting out of the roller coaster in Santa Cruz, and Elsie Doublebottom had made a novena and wasn't much good for anything else. The men from the sardine fleet, loaded with dough, were in and out all afternoon. They sail at dark and fish all night, so they must play in the afternoon. In the evening the soldiers of the new regiment came down and stood around playing the musical-box and drinking Coca-Cola and sizing up the girls for the time when they would be paid. Dora was having trouble with her income-tax, for she was entangled in that curious enigma which said the business was illegal and then taxed her for it. In addition to everything else there were the regulars – the steady customers who had been coming down for years, the labourers from the gravel-pits, the riders from the ranches, the railroad men who came in the front door, and the city officials and prominent business men who came in the rear entrance by the tracks and who had little chintz sitting-rooms assigned to them.

All in all it was a terrific month and right in the middle of it the influenza epidemic had to break out. It came to the whole town. Mrs Talbot and her daughter of the San

Carlos Hotel had it. Tom Work had it. Benjamin Peabody and his wife had it. Excelentisima Maria Antonia Field had it. The whole Gross family came down with it.

The doctors of Monterey – and there were enough of them to take care of the ordinary diseases, accidents, and neuroses – were running crazy. They had more business than they could do among clients who, if they didn't pay their bills, at least had the money to pay them. Cannery Row, which produces a tougher breed than the rest of the town, was late in contracting it, but finally it got them too. The schools were closed. There wasn't a house that hadn't feverish children and sick parents. It was not a deadly disease, as it was in 1917, but with children it had a tendency to go into the mastoids. The medical profession was very busy, and besides, Cannery Row was not considered a very good financial risk.

Now Doc of the Western Biological Laboratory had no right to practise medicine. It was not his fault that everyone in the Row came to him for medical advice. Before he knew it he found himself running from shanty to shanty taking temperatures, giving physics, borrowing and delivering blankets, and even taking food from house to house where mothers looked at him with inflamed eyes from their beds, and thanked him and put the full responsibility for their children's recovery on him. When a case got really out of hand he phoned a local doctor and sometimes one came, if it seemed to be an emergency. But to the families it was all emergency. Doc didn't get much sleep. He lived on beer and canned sardines. In Lee Chong's where he went to get beer he met Dora, who was there to buy a pair of nail clippers.

'You look done in,' Dora said.

'I am,' Doc admitted. 'I haven't had any sleep for about a week.'

'I know,' said Dora, 'I hear it's bad. Comes at a bad time too.'

'Well, we haven't lost anybody yet,' said Doc. 'But there

are some awful sick kids. The Ransel kids have all developed mastoiditis.'

'Is there anything I can do?' Dora asked.

Doc said: 'You know there is. People get so scared and helpless. Take the Ransels – they're scared to death and they're scared to be alone. If you, or some of the girls, could just sit with them.'

Dora, who was soft as a mouse's belly, could be as hard as carborundum. She went back to the Bear Flag and organized it for service. It was a bad time for her, but she did it. The Greek cook made a ten-gallon cauldron of strong soup and kept it full and kept it strong. The girls tried to keep up their business, but they went in shifts to sit with the families, and they carried pots of soup when they went. Doc was in almost constant demand. Dora consulted him and detailed the girls where he suggested. And all the time the business at the Bear Flag was booming. The musical-box never stopped playing. The men of the fishing fleet and the soldiers stood in line. And the girls did their work and then they took their pots of soup and went to sit with the Ransels, with the McCarthys, with the Ferrias. The girls slipped out the back door, and sometimes staying with the sleeping children the girls dropped to sleep in their chairs. They didn't use make-up for work any more. They didn't have to. Dora herself said she could have used the total membership of the old ladies' home. It was the busiest time the girls at the Bear Flag could remember. Everyone was glad when it was over.

CHAPTER XVII

In spite of his friendliness and his friends Doc was a lonely and a set-apart man. Mack probably noticed it more than anybody. In a group, Doc seemed always alone. When the lights were on and the curtains drawn, and the Gregorian music played on the great phonograph, Mack used to look down on the laboratory from the Palace Flophouse. He knew Doc had a girl in there, but Mack used to get a dreadful feeling of loneliness out of it. Even in the dear close contact with a girl Mack felt that Doc would be lonely. Doc was a night crawler. The lights were on in the lab all night and yet he seemed to be up in the daytime too. And the great shrouds of music came out of the lab at any time of the day or night. Sometimes when it was all dark and when it seemed that sleep had come at last, the diamond-true child voices of the Sistine Choir would come from the windows of the laboratory.

Doc had to keep up his collecting. He tried to get to the good tides along the coast. The sea rocks and the beaches were his stock pile. He knew where everything was when he wanted it. All the articles of his trade were filed away on the coast, sea cradles here, octopi here, tubs worms in another place, sea pansies in another. He knew where to get them, but he could not go for them exactly when he wanted. For Nature locked up the items and released them only occasionally. Doc had to know not only the tides, but when a particular low tide was good in a particular place. When such a low tide occurred, he packed his collecting tools in his car, he packed his jars, his bottles, his plates and preservatives and he went to the beach or reef or rock ledge where the animals he needed were stored.

Now he had an order for small octopi and the nearest place to get them was the boulder-strewn inter-tidal zone at La Jolla, between Los Angeles and San Diego. It meant a five-hundred-mile drive each way and his arrival had to coincide with the retreating waters.

The little octopi live among the boulders embedded in sand. Being timid and young, they prefer a bottom on which there are many caves and little crevices and lumps of mud where they may hide from predators and protect themselves from the waves. But on the same flat there are millions of sea cradles. While filling a definite order for octopi, Doc could replenish his stock of the cradles.

Low tide was 5.17 a.m. on a Thursday. If Doc left Monterey on Wednesday morning he could be there easily in time for the tide on Thursday. He would have taken someone with him for company, but quite by accident everyone was away or was busy. Mack and the boys were up Carmel Valley collecting frogs. Three young women he knew and would have enjoyed as companions had jobs and couldn't get away in the middle of the week. Henri the painter was occupied, for Holman's Department Store had employed not a flag-pole sitter, but a flag-pole skater. On a tall mast on top of the store he had a little round platform and there he was on skates going round and round. He had been there three days and three nights. He was out to set a new record for being on skates on a platform. The previous record was 127 hours, so he had some time to go. Henri had taken up his post across the street at Red Williams' petrol station. Henri was fascinated. He thought of doing a huge abstraction called Substratum Dream of a Flag-pole Skater. Henri couldn't leave town while the skater was up there. He protested that there were philosophic implications in flag-pole skating that no one had touched. Henri sat in a chair, leaned back against the lattice which concealed the door of the men's toilet at Red Williams'. He kept his eye on the eyrie skating platform and obviously he couldn't go with Doc to La Jolla. Doc had to go alone because the tide would not wait.

Early in the morning he got his things together. Personal things went in a small satchel. Another satchel held instruments and syringes. Having packed, he combed and trimmed his brown beard, saw that his pencils were in his shirt pocket, and his magnifying glass attached to his lapel. He packed the trays, bottles, glass plates, preservatives, rubber-boots, and a blanket into the back of his car. He worked through the pearly time, washed three days' dishes, put the garbage into the surf. He closed the doors, but did not lock them, and by nine o'clock was on his way.

It took Doc longer to go places than other people. He didn't drive fast and he stopped and ate hamburgers very often. Driving up to Lighthouse Avenue he waved at a dog that looked round and smiled at him. In Monterey before he even started, he felt hungry and stopped at Herman's for a hamburger and beer. While he ate his sandwich and sipped his beer, a lot of conversation came back to him. Blaisedell, the poet, had said to him: 'You love beer so much. I'll bet some day you'll go in and order a beer milk-shake.' It was a simple piece of foolery, but it had bothered Doc ever since. He wondered what a beer milk-shake would taste like. The idea gagged him, but he couldn't let it alone. It cropped up every time he had a glass of beer. Would it curdle the milk? Would you add sugar? It was like a shrimp ice-cream. Once the thing got into your head you couldn't forget it. He finished his sandwich and paid Herman. He purposely didn't look at the milk-shake machines lined up so shiny against the back wall. If a man ordered a beer milk-shake, he thought, he'd better do it in a town where he wasn't known. But then, a man with a beard, ordering a beer milk-shake in a town where he wasn't known – they might call the police. A man with a beard was always a little suspect anyway. You couldn't say you wore a beard because you like a beard. People didn't like you for telling the truth. You had to say you had a scar, so you couldn't shave. Once when Doc was at the University of Chicago he had loved trouble and he had worked too hard. He thought it would be nice to take a very long walk. He put on a little knapsack and he walked through Indiana and Kentucky and North Carolina and Georgia, clear to Florida. He walked among farmers and mountain people, among the swamp people and fishermen. And everywhere people asked him why he was walking through the country.

Because he loved true things he tried to explain. He said he was nervous and besides he wanted to see the country, smell the ground and look at grass and birds and trees, to savour the country, and there was no other way to do it save on foot. And people didn't like him for telling the truth. They scowled, or shook and tapped their heads, they laughed as though they knew it was a lie and they appreciated a liar. And some, afraid for their daughters or their pigs, told him to move on, to get along, just not to stop near their place if he knew what was good for him.

And so he stopped trying to tell the truth. He said he was doing it on a bet – that he stood to win a hundred dollars. Everyone liked him then and believed him. They asked him in to dinner and gave him a bed and they put lunches up for him and wished him good luck and thought he was a hell of a fine fellow. Doc still loved true things, but he knew it was not a general love and it could be a very dangerous mistress.

Doc didn't stop in Salinas for a hamburger. But he stopped in Gonzales, in King City, and in Paso Robles. He had hamburger and beer at Santa Maria – two in Santa Maria, because it was a long pull from there to Santa Barbara. In Santa Barbara he had soup, lettuce and string-bean salad, pot roast and mashed potatoes, pineapple-pie and blue cheese and coffee, and after that he filled the petrol tank and went to the toilet. While the service station checked his oil and tyres, Doc washed his face and combed his beard and when he came back to the car a number of potential hitch-hikers were waiting.

'Going south, Mister?'

Doc travelled on the highways a good deal. He was an old hand. You have to pick your hitch-hikers very carefully. It's best to get an experienced one, for he relapses into silence. But the new ones try to pay for their ride by being interesting. Doc had had a leg talked off by some of these. Then after you have made up your mind about the one you want to take, you protect yourself by saying you aren't going far. If your man turns out too much for you, you can drop him. On the other hand, you may be just lucky and get a man very much worth knowing. Doc made a quick survey of the line and chose his company, a thin-faced salesman-like man in a blue suit. He had deep lines beside his mouth and dark brooding eyes.

He looked at Doc with dislike. 'Going south, Mister?'

'Yes,' said Doc, 'a little way.'

'Mind taking me along?'

'Get in!' said Doc.

When they got to Ventura it was pretty soon after the heavy dinner, so Doc only stopped for beer. The hitch-hiker hadn't spoken once. Doc pulled up at a roadside stand.

'Want some beer?'

'No,' said the hitch-hiker. 'And I don't mind saying I think it's not a very good idea to drive under the influence of alcohol. It's none of my business what you do with your own life, but in this case you've got an automobile, and that can be a murderous weapon in the hands of a drunken driver.'

At the beginning Doc had been slightly startled. 'Get out of the car,' he said softly.

'What?'

'I'm going to punch you on the nose,' said Doc, 'if you

aren't out of this car before I count ten. One – two – three . . .'

The man fumbled at the door catch and backed hurriedly out of the car. But once outside he howled: 'I'm going to find an officer. I'm going to have you arrested.'

Doc opened the box on the dashboard and took out a monkey wrench. His guest saw the gesture and walked hurriedly away.

Doc walked angrily to the counter of the stand.

The waitress, a blonde beauty with just the hint of a goitre, smiled at him. 'What'll it be?'

'Beer milk-shake,' said Doc.

'What?'

Well here it was and what the hell. Might just as well get it over with now as some time later.

The blonde asked: 'Are you kidding?'

Doc knew wearily that he couldn't explain, couldn't tell the truth. 'I've got a bladder complaint,' he said. 'Bipalychaetsonectomy, the doctors call it. I'm supposed to drink a *beer milk-shake*. Doctor's orders.'

The blonde smiled reassuringly. 'Oh! I thought you was kidding,' she said archly. 'You tell me how to make it. I didn't know you was sick.'

'Very sick,' said Doc, 'and due to be sicker. Put in some milk, and add half a bottle of beer. Give me the other half in a glass – no sugar in the milk-shake.' When she served it, he tasted it wryly. And it wasn't so bad – it just tasted like stale beer and milk.

'It sounds awful,' said the blonde.

'It's not so bad when you get used to it,' said Doc. 'I've been drinking it for seventeen years.'

CHAPTER XVIII

Doc had driven slowly. It was late afternoon when he stopped in Ventura, so late in fact that when he stopped in Carpentaria he only had a cheese sandwich and went to the toilet. Besides, he intended to get a good dinner in Los Angeles, and it was dark when he got there. He drove on through and stopped at a big Chicken-in-the-Rough place he knew about. And there he had fried chicken, julienne potatoes, hot biscuits and honey, and a piece of pineapple-pie and blue cheese. And here he filled his thermos-bottle with hot coffee, had them make up six ham sandwiches, and bought two quarts of beer for breakfast.

It was not so interesting driving at night. No dogs to see, only the highway lighted with his headlights. Doc speeded up to finish the trip. It was about two o'clock when he got to La Jolla. He drove through the town and down to the cliff below which his tidal flat lay. There he stopped the car, ate a sandwich, drank some beer, turned out the lights, and curled up in the seat to sleep.

He didn't need a clock. He had been working in a tidal pattern so long that he could feel a tide change in his sleep. In the dawn he awakened, looked out through the windshield, and saw that the water was already retreating down the bouldery flat. He drank some hot coffee, ate three sandwiches, and had a quart of beer.

The tide goes out imperceptibly. The boulders show and seem to rise up and the ocean recedes, leaving little pools, leaving wet weed and moss and sponge, iridescence and brown and blue and China red. On the bottoms lie the incredible refuse of the sea, shells broken and chipped and bits of skeleton, claws, the whole sea bottom a fantastic cemetery on which the living scamper and scramble.

Doc pulled on his rubber-boots and set his rain hat fussily. He took his buckets and jars and his crowbar, and put his sandwiches in one pocket and his thermos-bottle in another pocket, and he went down the cliff to the tidal flat. Then he worked down the flat after the retreating sea. He turned over the boulders with his crowbar and now and then his hand darted quickly into the standing-water and brought out a little angry squirming octopus, which blushed with rage and spat ink on his hand. Then he dropped it into a jar of sea water with the others, and usually the newcomer was so angry that it attacked its fellows.

It was good hunting that day. He got twenty-two little octopi. And he picked off several hundred sea cradles and put them in his wooden bucket. As the tide moved out he followed it, while the morning came and the sun arose. The flat extended out two hundred yards and then there was a line of heavy weed-crusted rocks before it dropped off to deep water. Doc worked out to the barrier edge. He had about what he wanted now and the rest of the time he looked under stones, leaned down, and peered into the tide pools, with their brilliant mosaics and their scuttling, bubbling life. And he came at last to the outer barrier, where the long leathery brown algae hung down into the water. Red starfish clustered on the rocks, and the sea pulsed up and down against the barrier, waiting to get in again. Between two weeded rocks on the barrier Doc saw a flash of white under water and then the floating weed covered it. He climbed to the place over the slippery rocks, held himself firmly, and gently reached down and parted the brown algae. Then he grew rigid. A girl's face looked up at him, a pretty, pale girl with dark hair. The eyes were open and clear and the face was firm and the hair washed gently about her head. The body was out of sight, caught in the crevice. The lips were slightly parted and the teeth showed, and on the face was only comfort and rest. Just under water it was and the clear water made it very beautiful. It seemed to Doc that he looked at it for many minutes, and the face burned into his picture memory.

Very slowly he raised his hand and let the brown weed float back and cover the face. Doc's heart pounded deeply and his throat felt tight. He picked up his bucket and his jars and his crowbar and went slowly over the slippery rocks back toward the beach.

And the girl's face went ahead of him. He sat down on the beach in the coarse dry sand and pulled off his boots. In the jar the little octopi were huddled up, each keeping as far as possible from the others. Music sounded in Doc's ears, a high thin piercingly sweet flute carrying a melody he could never remember, and against this, a pounding surf-like wood-wind section. The flute went up into regions beyond the hearing range and even there it carried its unbelievable melody. Goose pimples came out on Doc's arms. He shivered and his eyes were wet the way they get in the focus of great beauty. The girl's eyes had been grey and clear and the dark hair floated, drifted lightly over the face. The picture was set for all time. He sat there while the first little spout of water came over the reef, bringing the returning tide. He sat there hearing the music, while the sea crept in again over the bouldery flat. His hand tapped out the rhythm, and the terrifying flute played in his brain. The eyes were grey and the mouth smiled a little or seemed to catch its breath in ecstasy.

A voice seemed to awaken him. A man stood over him. 'Been fishing?'

'No, collecting.'

'Well – what are them things?'

'Baby octopi.'

'You mean devil-fish? I didn't know there was any there. I've lived here all my life.'

'You've got to look for them,' said Doc listlessly.

'Say,' said the man, 'aren't you feeling well? You look sick.'

The flute climbed again and plucked cellos sounded below and the sea crept in and in toward the beach. Doc shook off the music, shook off the face, shook the chill out of his body. 'Is there a police station near?'

'Up in town. Why, what's wrong?'

'There's a body out on the reef.'

'Where?'

'Right out there – wedged between two rocks. A girl.'

'Say . . .' said the man. 'You get a bounty for finding a body. I forget how much.'

Doc stood up and gathered his equipment. 'Will you report it? I'm not feeling well.'

'Give you a shock, did it? Is it – bad? Rotten or eat up?'

Doc turned away. 'You take the bounty,' he said. 'I don't want it.' He started toward the car. Only the tiniest piping of the flute sounded in his head.

CHAPTER XIX

PROBABLY nothing in the way of promotion Holman's Department Store ever did attracted so much favourable comment as the engagement of the flag-pole skater. Day after day, there he was up on his little round platform skating round and round, and at night he could be seen up there too, dark against the sky, so that everybody knew he didn't come down. It was generally agreed, however, that a steel rod came up through the centre of the platform at night and he strapped himself to it. But he didn't sit down and no one minded the steel rod. People came from Jamesburg to see him and from down the coast as far as Grimes Point. Salinas people came over in droves and the Farmers Mercantile of that town put in a bid for the next appearance when the skater could attempt to break his own record and thus give the new world's record to Salinas. Since there weren't many flag-pole skaters and since this one was by far the best, he had for the last year gone about breaking his own world's record.

Holman's was delighted about the venture. They had a white sale, a remnant sale, an aluminium sale, and a crockery sale all going at the same time. Crowds of people stood in the street watching the lone man on his platform.

His second day up, he sent down word that someone was shooting at him with an air-gun. The display department used its head. It figured the angles and located the offender. It was old Doctor Merrivale, hiding behind the curtains of his office, plugging away with a Daisy air-rifle. They didn't denounce him and he promised to stop. He was very prominent in the Masonic Lodge.

Henri the painter kept his chair at Red Williams' service station. He worked out every possible philosophic approach to the situation and came to the conclusion that he would have to build a platform at home and try it himself. Everyone in the town was more or less affected by the skater. Trade fell off out of sight of him and got better the nearer you came to Holman's. Mack and the boys went up and looked for a moment and then went back to the Palace. They couldn't see that it made much sense.

Holman's set up a double bed in their windows. When the skater broke the world's record he was going to come down and sleep right in the window without taking off his skates. The trade name of the mattress was on a little card at the foot of the bed.

Now in the whole town there was interest and discussion about this sporting event, but the most interesting question of all and the one that bothered the whole town was never spoken of. No one mentioned it, and yet it was there haunting everyone. Mrs Trolat wondered about it as she came out of the Scotch bakery with a bag of sweet buns. Mr Hall in men's furnishings wondered about it. The three Willoughby girls giggled whenever they thought of it. But no one had the courage to bring it into the open.

Richard Frost, a highly-strung and brilliant young man, worried about it more than anyone else. It haunted him. Wednesday night he worried and Thursday night he fidgeted. Friday night he got drunk and had a fight with his wife. She cried for a while and then pretended to be asleep. She heard him slip from bed and go into the kitchen. He was getting another drink. And then she heard him dress quietly and go out. She cried some more then. It was very late. Mrs Frost was sure he was going down to Dora's Bear Flag.

Richard walked sturdily down the hill through the pines until he came to Lighthouse Avenue. He turned left and went up toward Holman's. He had the bottle in his pocket and just before he came to the store he took one more slug of it. The street lights were turned down low. The town was deserted. Not a soul moved. Richard stood in the middle of the street and looked up.

Dimly on top of the high mast he could see the lonely figure of the skater. He took another drink. He cupped his hands and called huskily: 'Hey!' There was no answer. 'Hey!' he called louder, and looked around to see if the cops had come out of their place beside the bank.

Down from the sky came a surly reply: 'What do you want?'

Richard cupped his hands again. 'How – how do you – go to the toilet?'

'I've got a can up here,' said the voice.

Richard turned and walked back the way he had come. He walked along Lighthouse and up through the pines and he came to his house and let himself in. As he undressed he

fe was awake. She bubbled a little when she was
ot into bed and she made room for him.
...s got a can up there,' Richard said.

CHAPTER XX

In mid-morning the Model T truck rolled triumphantly
home to Cannery Row and hopped the gutter and creaked
up through the weeds to its place behind Lee Chong's. The
boys blocked up the front wheels, drained what petrol was
left into a five-gallon can, took their frogs, and went wearily
home to the Palace Flophouse. Then Mack made a cere-
monious visit to Lee Chong while the boys got a fire going
in the big stove. Mack thanked Lee with dignity for lending
the truck. He spoke of the great success of the trip, of the
hundreds of frogs taken. Lee smiled shyly and waited for
the inevitable.

'We're in the chips,' Mack said enthusiastically. 'Doc
pays us a nickel a frog and we got about a thousand.'

Lee nodded. The price was standard. Everybody knew
that.

'Doc's away,' said Mack. 'Jesus, is he gonna be happy
when he sees all them frogs.'

Lee nodded again. He knew Doc was away and he also
knew where the conversation was going.

'Say, by the way,' said Mack as though he had just
thought of it. 'We're a little bit short right now . . .' He
managed to make it sound like a very unusual situation.

'No whisky,' said Lee Chong, and he smiled.

Mack was outraged. 'What would we want whisky for?
Why, we got a gallon of the finest whisky you ever laid a lip

over – a whole full God-damned-running-over gallon. By the way,' he continued, 'I and the boys would like to have you just step up for a snort with us. They told me to ask you.'

In spite of himself Lee smiled with pleasure. They wouldn't offer it if they didn't have it.

'No,' said Mack, 'I'll lay it on the line. I and the boys are pretty short and we're pretty hungry. You know the price of frogs is twenty for a buck. Now Doc is away and we're hungry. So what we thought is this. We don't want to see you lose nothing, so we'll make over to you twenty-five frogs for a buck. You got a five-frog profit there and nobody loses his shirt.'

'No,' said Lee. 'No money.'

'Well, hell, Lee, all we need is a little groceries. I'll tell you what – we want to give Doc a little party when he gets back. We got plenty of liquor, but we'd like to get maybe some steaks, and stuff like that. He's such a nice guy. Hell, when your wife had that bad tooth, who give her the laudanum?'

Mack had him. Lee was indebted to Doc – deeply indebted. What Lee was having trouble comprehending was how his indebtedness to Doc made it necessary that he give credit to Mack.

'We don't want you to have like a mortgage on frogs,' Mack went on. 'We will actually deliver right into your hands twenty-five frogs for every buck of groceries you let us have and you can come to the party too.'

Lee's mind nosed over the proposition like a mouse in a cheese cupboard. He could find nothing wrong with it. The whole thing was legitimate. Frogs *were* cash as far as Doc was concerned, the price was standard, and Lee had a double profit. He had his five-frog margin and also he had the grocery mark-up. The whole thing hinged on whether they actually had any frogs.

'We go see flog,' Lee said at last.

In front of the Palace he had a drink of the whisky, inspected the damp sacks of frogs, and agreed to the transaction. He stipulated, however, that he would take no dead frogs. Now Mack counted fifty frogs into a can and walked back to the grocery with Lee and got two dollars' worth of bacon and eggs and bread.

Lee, anticipating a brisk business, brought a big packing-case out and put it into the vegetable department. He emptied the fifty frogs into it and covered it with a wet gunny-sack to keep his charges happy.

And business was brisk. Eddie sauntered down and bought two frogs' worth of Bull Durham. Jones was outraged a little later when the price of Coca-Cola went up from one to two frogs. In fact bitterness arose as the day wore on and prices went up. Steak, for instance – the very best steak shouldn't have been more than ten frogs a pound, but Lee set it at twelve and a half. Canned peaches were sky high, eight frogs for a No 2 can. Lee had a stranglehold on the consumers. He was pretty sure that the Thrift Market or Holman's would not approve of this new monetary system. If the boys wanted steak, they knew they had to pay Lee's prices. Feeling ran high when Hazel, who had coveted a pair of yellow silk arm-bands for a long time, was told that if he didn't want to pay thirty-five frogs for them he could go somewhere else. The poison of greed was already creeping into the innocent and laudable merchandising agreement. Bitterness was piling up. But in Lee's packing-case the frogs were piling up too.

Financial bitterness could not eat too deeply into Mack and the boys, for they were not mercantile men. They did not measure their joy in goods sold, their egos in bank balances, nor their loves in what they cost. While they were mildly irritated that Lee was taking them for an economic ride or perhaps hop, two dollars' worth of bacon and eggs was in their stomachs lying right on top of a fine slug of whisky and right on top of the breakfast was another slug

of whisky. And they sat in their own chairs in their own
house and watched Darling learning to drink canned milk
out of a sardine can. Darling was and was destined to remain a very happy dog, for in the group of five men there
were five distinct theories of dog training, theories which
clashed so that Darling never got any training at all. From
the first she was a precocious bitch. She slept on the bed of
the man who had given her the last bribe. They really stole
for her sometimes. They wooed her away from one another.
Occasionally all five agreed that things had to change and
that Darling must be disciplined, but in the discussion of
method the intention invariably drifted away. They were in
love with her. They found the little puddles she left on the
floor charming. They bored all their acquaintances with her
cuteness and they would have killed her with food if in the
end she hadn't had better sense than they.

Jones made her a bed in the bottom of the grandfather
clock, but Darling never used it. She slept with one or
another of them as the fancy moved her. She chewed the
blankets, tore the mattresses, sprayed the feathers out of the
pillows. She coquetted and played her owners against one
another. They thought she was wonderful. Mack intended
to teach her tricks and go in vaudeville and he didn't even
house-break her.

They sat in the afternoon, smoking, digesting, considering, and now and then having a delicate drink from the jug.
And each time they warned that they must not take too
much, for it was to be for Doc. They must not forget that
for a minute.

'What time you figure he'll be back?' Eddie asked.

'Usually gets in about eight or nine o'clock,' said Mack.
'Now we got to figure when we're going to give it. I think
we ought to give it tonight.'

'Sure,' the others agreed.

'Maybe he might be tired,' Hazel suggested. 'That's a
long drive.'

'Hell,' said Jones, 'nothing rests you like a good party. I've been so dog-tired my pants was draggin' and then I've went to a party and felt fine.'

'We got to do some real thinkin',' said Mack. 'Where we going to give it – here?'

'Well, Doc, he likes his music. He's always got his phonograph going at a party. Maybe he'd be more happy if we give it over at his place.'

'You got something there,' said Mack. 'But I figure it ought to be like a surprise party. And how we going to make like it's a party and not just bringin' over a jug of whisky?'

'How about decorations?' Hughie suggested. 'Like Fourth of July or Halloween.'

Mack's eyes looked off into space and his lips were parted. He could see it all. 'Hughie,' he said. 'I think you got something there. I never would of thought you could do it, but by God you really rang a duck that time.' His voice grew mellow and his eyes looked into the future. 'I can just see it,' he said. 'Doc comes home. He's tired. He drives up. The place is all lit up. He thinks somebody's broke in. He goes up the stairs, and by God the place has got the hell decorated out of it. There's crêpe paper and there's favours and a big cake. Jesus, he'd know it was a party then. And it wouldn't be no little mouse fart party neither. And we're kind of hiding so for a minute he don't know who done it. And then we come out yelling. Can't you see his face? By God, Hughie, I don't know how you thought of it.'

Hughie blushed. His conception had been much more conservative, based in fact on the New Year's party at 'La Ida', but if it was going to be like that, why Hughie was willing to take credit. 'I just thought it would be nice,' he said.

'Well, it's a pretty nice thing,' said Mack, 'and I don't mind saying when the surprise kind of wears off, I'm going to tell Doc who thought it up.' They leaned back and considered the thing. And in their minds the decorated laboratory looked like the conservatory at the Hotel del Monte.

They had a couple more drinks, just to savour the plan.

Lee Chong kept a very remarkable store. For instance, most stores buy yellow-and-black crêpe paper and black paper cats, masks and papier-mâché pumpkins in October. There is a brisk business for Halloween and then these items disappear. Maybe they are sold or thrown out, but you can't buy them, say, in June. The same is true of Fourth of July equipment, flags and bunting and sky-rockets. Where are they in January? Gone – no one knows where. This was not Lee Chong's way. You could buy Valentines in November at Lee Chong's, shamrocks, hatchets, and paper cherry-trees in August. He had fire-crackers he had laid up in 1920. One of the mysteries was where he kept his stock since his was not a very large store. He had bathing-suits he had bought when long skirts and black stockings and head bandanas were in style. He had bicycle clips and tatting shuttles and Mah Jong sets. He had badges that said 'Remember the Maine' and felt pennants commemorating 'Fighting Bob'. He had mementos of the Panama Pacific International Exposition of 1915 – little towers of jewels. And there was one other unorthodoxy in Lee's way of doing business. He never had a sale, never reduced a price, and never remaindered. An article that cost thirty cents in 1912 still was thirty cents, although mice and moths might seem to some to have reduced its value. But there was no question about it. If you wanted to decorate a laboratory in a general way, not being specific about the season but giving the impression of a cross between Saturnalia and a pageant of the Flags of all Nations, Lee Chong's was the place to go for your stuff.

Mack and the boys knew that, but Mack said: 'Where we going to get a big cake? Lee hasn't got nothing but them little bakery cakes.'

Hughie had been so successful before he tried again. 'Why'n't Eddie bake a cake?' he suggested. 'Eddie used to be fry cook at the San Carlos for a while.'

The instant enthusiasm for the idea drove from Eddie's

brain the admission that he had never baked a cake.

Mack put it on a sentimental basis besides. 'It would mean more to Doc,' he said. 'It wouldn't be like no God damned old soggy bought cake. It would have some heart in it.'

As the afternoon and the whisky went down the enthusiasm rose. There were endless trips to Lee Chong's. The frogs were gone from one sack and Lee's packing-case was getting crowded. By six o'clock they had finished the gallon of whisky and were buying half-pints of Old Tennis Shoes at fifteen frogs a crack, but the pile of decorating materials was heaped on the floor of the Palace Flophouse – miles of crêpe paper commemorating every holiday in vogue and some that had been abandoned.

Eddie watched his stove like a mother hen. He was baking a cake in a wash-basin. The recipe was guaranteed not to fail by the company which made the shortening. But from the first the cake had acted strangely. When the batter was completed it writhed and panted as though animals were squirming and crawling inside it. Once in the oven it put up a bubble like a baseball which grew tight and shiny and then collapsed with a hissing sound. This left such a crater that Eddie made a new batch of batter and filled in the hole. And now the cake was behaving very curiously, for while the bottom was burning and sending out a black smoke the top was rising and falling glueyly with a series of little explosions.

When Eddie finally put it out to cool, it looked like one of Bel Geddes's miniatures of a battlefield on a lava bed.

This cake was not fortunate, for while the boys were decorating the laboratory Darling ate what she could of it, was sick on it, and finally curled up in its still warm dough and went to sleep.

But Mack and the boys had taken the crêpe paper, the masks, the broomsticks and paper pumpkins, the red, white and blue bunting, and moved over the lot and across the street to the laboratory. They disposed of the last of the frogs for a quart of Old Tennis Shoes and two gallons of 49-cent wine.

'Doc is very fond of wine,' said Mack. 'I think he likes it even better than whisky.'

Doc never locked the laboratory. He went on the theory that anyone who really wanted to break in could easily do it, that people were essentially honest, and that finally there wasn't much the average person would want to steal there, anyway. The valuable things were books and records, surgical instruments and optical glass and such things that a practical working burglar wouldn't look at twice. His theory had been sound as far as burglars, snatch thieves, and kleptomaniacs were concerned, but it had been completely ineffective regarding his friends. Books were often 'borrowed'. No can of beans ever survived his absence, and on several occasions, returning late, he had found guests in his bed.

The boys piled the decorations in the ante-room and then Mack stopped them. 'What's going to make Doc happiest?' he asked.

'The party!' said Hazel.

'No,' said Mack.

'The decorations?' Hughie suggested. He felt responsible for the decorations.

'No,' said Mack, 'the frogs. That's going to make him feel best of all. And maybe by the time he gets here, Lee Chong might be closed and he can't even see his frogs until tomorrow. No, sir,' Mack cried. 'Them frogs ought to be right here, right in the middle of the room with a piece of bunting on it and a sign that says: "Welcome Home, Doc".'

The committee which visited Lee met with stern opposition. All sorts of possibilities suggested themselves to his suspicious brain. It was explained that he was going to be at the party so he could watch his property, that no one questioned that they were his. Mack wrote out a paper transferring the frogs to Lee in case there should be any question.

When his protests weakened a little they carried the packing-case over to the laboratory, tacked red, white, and blue bunting over it, lettered the big sign with iodine on a card, and they started the decorating from there. They had finished the whisky by now and they really felt in a party mood. They criss-crossed the crêpe paper, and put the pumpkins up. Passers-by in the street joined the party and rushed over to Lee's to get more to drink. Lee Chong joined the party for a while, but his stomach was notoriously weak and he got sick and had to go home. At eleven o'clock they fried the steaks and ate them. Someone digging through the records found an album of Count Basie and the great phonograph roared out. The noise could be heard from the boatworks to 'La Ida'. A group of customers from the Bear Flag mistook Western Biological for a rival house and charged up the stairs whooping with joy. They were evicted by the outraged hosts, but only after a long, happy, and bloody battle that took out the front door and broke two windows. The crashing of jars was unpleasant. Hazel going through the kitchen to the toilet tipped the frying-pan of hot grease on himself and the floor and was badly burned.

At one-thirty a drunk wandered in and passed a remark which was considered insulting to Doc. Mack hit him a clip which is still remembered and discussed. The man rose off his feet, described a small arc, and crashed through the packing-case in among the frogs. Someone trying to change a record dropped the tone arm down and broke the crystal.

No one has studied the psychology of a dying party. It may be raging, howling, boiling, and then a fever sets in and a little silence and then quickly quickly it is gone, the guests go home or go to sleep or wander away to some other affair and they leave a dead body.

The lights blazed in the laboratory. The front door hung sideways by one hinge. The floor was littered with broken glass. Phonograph records, some broken, some only nicked, were strewn about. The plates with pieces of steak ends and coagulating grease were on the floor, on top of the bookcases, under the bed. Whisky-glasses lay sadly on their sides.

Someone trying to climb the bookcases had pulled out a whole section of books and spilled them in broken-backed confusion on the floor. And it was empty, it was over.

Through the broken end of the packing-case a frog hopped and sat feeling the air for danger, and then another joined him. They could smell the fine, damp, cool air coming in the door and in through the broken windows. One of them sat on the fallen card which said: 'Welcome Home, Doc.' And then the two hopping timidly toward the door.

For quite a while a little river of frogs hopped down the steps, a swirling, moving river. For quite a while Cannery Row crawled with frogs – was overrun with frogs. A taxi which brought a very late customer to the Bear Flag squashed five frogs in the street. But well before dawn they had all gone. Some found the sewer and some worked their way up the hill to the reservoir and some went into culverts and some only hid among the weeds in the vacant lot.

And the lights blazed in the quiet empty laboratory.

CHAPTER XXI

In the back room of the laboratory the white rats in their cages ran and skittered and squeaked. In the corner of a separate cage a mother rat lay over her litter of blind, naked children and let them suckle and the mother stared about nervously and fiercely.

In the rattlesnake cage the snakes lay with their chins resting on their own coils and they stared straight ahead out of their scowling dusty black eyes. In another cage a Gila monster with a skin like a beaded bag reared slowly up and clawed heavily and sluggishly at the wire. The anemones in the aquaria blossomed open, with green and purple tentacles and pale green stomachs. The little sea-water pump whirred softly and the needles of driven water hissed into the tanks, forcing lines of bubbles under the surface.

It was the hour of the pearl. Lee Chong brought his gar-bage cans out to the kerb. The bouncer stood on the porch of the Bear Flag and scratched his stomach. Sam Malloy crawled out of the boiler and sat on his wood block and looked at the lightening east. Over on the rocks near Hop-kins Marine Station the sea-lions barked monotonously. The old Chinaman came up out of the sea with his dripping basket and flip-flapped up the hill.

Then a car turned into Cannery Row and Doc drove up to the front of the laboratory. His eyes were red-rimmed with fatigue. He moved slowly with tiredness. When the car had stopped, he sat still for a moment to let the road jumps get out of his nerves. Then he climbed out of the car. At his step on the stairs, the rattlesnakes ran out their tongues and listened with their waving forked tongues. The rats scam-pered madly about the cages. Doc climbed the stairs. He looked in wonder at the sagging door and at the broken window. The weariness seemed to go out of him. He stepped quickly inside. Then he went quickly from room to room, stepping round the broken glass. He bent down quickly and picked up a smashed phonograph record and looked at its title.

In the kitchen the spilled grease had turned white on the floor. Doc's eyes flamed red with anger. He sat down on his couch and his head settled between his shoulders and his body weaved a little in his rage. Suddenly he jumped up and turned on the power in his great phonograph. He put on a record and put down the arm. Only a hissing roar came from the loud-speaker. He lifted the arm, stopped the turn-table, and sat down on the couch again.

On the stairs there were bumbling uncertain footsteps and

through the door came Mack. His face was red. He stood uncertainly in the middle of the room. 'Doc . . .' he said – 'I and the boys . . .'

For the moment Doc hadn't seemed to see him. Now he leaped to his feet. Mack shuffled backward. 'Did you do this?'

'Well, I and the boys . . .' Doc's small hard fist whipped out and splashed against Mack's mouth. Doc's eyes shone with a red animal rage. Mack sat down heavily on the floor. Doc's fist was hard and sharp. Mack's lips were split against his teeth and one front tooth bent sharply inward. 'Get up!' said Doc.

Mack lumbered to his feet. His hands were at his sides. Doc hit him again, a cold, calculated, punishing punch in the mouth. The blood spurted from Mack's lips and ran down his chin. He tried to lick his lips.

'Put up your hands. Fight, you son of a bitch,' Doc cried, and he hit him again and heard the crunch of breaking teeth.

Mack's head jolted, but he was braced now so he wouldn't fall. And his hands stayed at his side. 'Go ahead, Doc,' he said thickly through his broken lips. 'I got it coming.'

Doc's shoulders sagged with defeat. 'You son of a bitch,' he said bitterly. 'Oh, you dirty son of a bitch.' He sat down on the couch and looked at his cut knuckles.

Mack sat down in a chair and looked at him. Mack's eyes were wide and full of pain. He didn't even wipe away the blood that flowed down his chin. In Doc's head the mono-tonal opening of Monteverdi's *Hor ch' il Ciel e la Terra* began to form, the infinitely sad and resigned mourning of Petrarch for Laura. Doc saw Mack's broken mouth through the music, the music that was in his head and in the air. Mack sat perfectly still, almost as though he could hear the music too. Doc glanced at the place where the Monteverdi album was and then he remembered that the phonograph was broken.

He got to his feet. 'Go wash your face,' he said, and he

went out and down the stairs and across the street to Lee Chong's. Lee wouldn't look at him as he got two quarts of beer out of the ice-box. He took the money without saying anything. Doc walked across the street.

Mack was in the toilet cleaning his bloody face with wet paper towels. Doc opened a bottle and poured gently into a glass, holding it at an angle so that very little collar rose to the top. He filled a second tall glass and carried the two into the front room. Mack came back dabbing at his mouth with wet towelling. Doc indicated the beer with his head. Now Mack opened his throat and poured down half the glass without swallowing. He sighed explosively and stared into the beer. Doc had already finished his glass. He brought the bottle in and filled both glasses again. He sat down on his couch.

'What happened?' he asked.

Mack looked at the floor and a drop of blood fell from his lips to his beer. He mopped his split lips again. 'I and the boys wanted to give you a party. We thought you'd be home last night.'

Doc nodded his head. 'I see.'

'She got out of hand,' said Mack. 'It don't do no good to say I'm sorry. I been sorry all my life. This ain't no new thing. It's always like this.' He swallowed deeply from his glass. 'I had a wife,' Mack said. 'Same thing. Ever'thing I done turned sour. She couldn't stand it any more. If I done a good thing it got poisoned up some way. If I give her a present they was something wrong with it. She only got hurt from me. She couldn't stand it no more. Same thing ever' place 'til I just got to clowning. I don't do nothin' but clown no more. Try to make the boys laugh.'

Doc nodded again. The music was sounding in his head again, complaint and resignation all in one. 'I know,' he said.

'I was glad when you hit me,' Mack went on. 'I thought to myself: "Maybe this will teach me. Maybe I'll remember this." But, hell, I won't remember nothin'. I won't learn nothin'. Doc,' Mack cried, 'the way I seen it, we was all happy and havin' a good time. You was glad because we was givin' you a party. And we was glad. The way I seen it, it was a good party.' He waved his hand at the wreckage on the floor. 'Same thing when I was married. I'd think her out and then – but it never come off that way.'

'I know,' said Doc. He opened the second quart of beer and poured the glasses full.

'Doc,' said Mack. 'I and the boys will clean up here – and we'll pay for the stuff that's broke. If it takes us five years we'll pay for it.'

Doc shook his head slowly and wiped the beer foam from his moustache. 'No,' he said, 'I'll clean it up. I know where everything goes.'

'We'll pay for it, Doc.'

'No you won't, Mack,' said Doc. 'You'll think about it and it'll worry you for quite a long time, but you won't pay for it. There's maybe three hundred dollars in broken museum glass. Don't say you'll pay for it. That will just keep you uneasy. It might be two or three years before you forgot about it and felt entirely easy again. And you wouldn't pay it, anyway.'

'I guess you're right,' said Mac. 'God damn it, I *know* you're right. What can we do?'

'I'm over it,' said Doc. 'Those socks in the mouth got it out of my system. Let's forget it.'

Mack finished his beer and stood up. 'So long, Doc,' he said.

'So long. Say, Mack – what happened to your wife?'

'I don't know,' said Mack. 'She went away.' He walked clumsily down the stairs and crossed over and walked up the lot and up the chicken walk to the Palace Flophouse. Doc watched his progress through the window. And then wearily he got a broom from behind the water-heater. It took him all day to clean up the mess.

CHAPTER XXII

HENRI the painter was not French and his name was not Henri. Also he was not really a painter. Henri had so steeped himself in stories of the Left Bank in Paris that he lived there although he had never been there. Feverishly he followed in periodicals the Dadaist movements and schisms, the strangely feminine jealousies and religiousness, the obscurantisms of the forming and breaking schools. Regularly he revolted against outworn techniques and materials. One season he threw out perspective. Another year he abandoned red, even as the mother of purple. Finally he gave up paint entirely. It is not known whether Henri was a good painter or not, for he threw himself so violently into movements that he had very little time left for painting of any kind.

About his painting there is some question. You couldn't judge very much from his productions in different coloured chicken feathers and nut-shells. But as a boat-builder he was superb. Henri was a wonderful craftsman. He had lived in a tent years ago when he started his boat and until galley and cabin were complete enough to move into. But once he was housed and dry he had taken his time on the boat. The boat was sculptured rather than built. It was thirty-five feet long and its lines were in a constant state of flux. For a while it had a clipper bow and a fan-tail like a destroyer. Another time it had looked vaguely like a caravel. Since Henri had no money, it sometimes took him months to find a plank or a piece of iron or a dozen brass screws. That was the way he wanted it, for Henri never wanted to finish his boat.

It sat among the pine-trees on a lot Henri rented for five dollars a year. This paid the taxes and satisfied the owner. The boat rested in a cradle on concrete foundations. A rope ladder hung over the side except when Henri was at home. Then he pulled up the rope ladder and only put it down when guests arrived. His little cabin had a wide padded seat that ran round three sides of the room. On this he slept and on this his guests sat. A table folded down when it was needed and a brass lamp hung from the ceiling. His galley was a marvel of compactness, but every item in it had been the result of months of thought and work.

Henri was swarthy and morose. He wore a beret long after other people abandoned them, he smoked a calabash pipe and his dark hair fell about his face. Henri had many friends whom he loosely classified as those who could feed him and those whom he had to feed. His boat had no name. Henri said he would name it when it was finished.

Henri had been living in and building his boat for ten years. During that time he had been married twice and had promoted a number of semi-permanent liaisons. And all of these young women had left him for the same reason. The seven-foot cabin was too small for two people. They resented bumping their heads when they stood up and they definitely felt the need for a toilet. Marine toilets obviously would not work in a shore-bound boat, and Henri refused to compromise with a spurious landsman's toilet. He and his friend of the moment had to stroll away among the pines. And one after another his loves left him.

Just after the girl he had called Alice left him, a very curious thing happened to Henri. Each time he was left alone, he mourned formally for a while, but actually he felt a sense of relief. He could stretch out in his little cabin. He could eat what he wanted. He was glad to be free of the endless female biologic functions for a while.

It had become his custom, each time he was deserted, to

buy a gallon of wine, to stretch out on the comfortably hard
bunk and get drunk. Sometimes he cried a little all by himself, but it was luxurious stuff and he usually had a wonder-
full feeling of well-being from it. He would read Rimbaud
aloud with a very bad accent, marvelling the while at his
fluid speech.

It was during one of his ritualistic mournings for the lost
Alice that the strange thing began to happen. It was night
and his lamp was burning and he had just barely begun to
get drunk when suddenly he knew he was no longer alone.
He let his eye wander cautiously up and across the cabin,
and there on the other side sat a devilish young man, a dark,
handsome young man. His eyes gleamed with cleverness
and spirit and energy and his teeth flashed. There was something very dear and yet very terrible in his face. And beside
him sat a golden-haired little boy, hardly more than a baby.
The man looked down at the baby and the baby looked
back and laughed delightedly as though something wonderful were about to happen. Then the man looked over at
Henri and smiled and he glanced back at the baby. From
his upper left vest pocket he took an old-fashioned straight
edged razor. He opened it and indicated the child with a
gesture of his head. He put a hand among the curls and the
baby laughed gleefully, and then the man tilted the chin
and cut the baby's throat and the baby went right on laughing. But Henri was howling with terror. It took him a long
time to realize that neither the man nor the baby was still
there.

Henri, when his shaking had subsided a little, rushed
out of his cabin, leaped over the side of the boat and
hurried away down the hill through the pines. He walked
for several hours and at last he walked down to Cannery
Row.

Doc was in the basement working on cats when Henri
burst in. Doc went on working while Henri told about it,
and when it was over Doc looked closely at him to see how

much actual fear and how much theatre was there. And it was mostly fear.

'Is it a ghost, do you think?' Henri demanded. 'Is it some reflection of something that has happened or is it some Freudian horror out of me, or am I completely nuts? I saw it, I tell you. It happened right in front of me as plainly as I see you.'

'I don't know,' said Doc.

'Well, will you come up with me, and see if it comes back?'

'No,' said Doc. 'If I saw it, it might be a ghost and it would scare me badly because I don't believe in ghosts. And if you saw it again and I didn't it would be a hallucination and you would be frightened.'

'But what am I going to do?' Henri asked. 'If I see it again I'll know what's going to happen and I'm sure I'll die. You see, he doesn't look like a murderer. He looks nice and the kid looks nice and neither of them give a damn. But he cut that baby's throat. I saw it.'

'I don't know,' said Doc. 'I'm not a psychiatrist or a witch-hunter and I'm not going to start now.'

A girl's voice called into the basement. 'Hi, Doc, can I come in?'

'Come along,' said Doc.

She was a rather pretty and a very alert girl.

Doc introduced her to Henri.

'He's got a problem,' said Doc. 'He either has a ghost or a terrible conscience and he doesn't know which. Tell her about it, Henri.'

Henri went over the story again and the girl's eyes sparkled.

'But that's horrible,' she said when he finished. 'I've never in my life even caught the smell of a ghost. Let's go back up and see if he comes again.'

Doc watched them go a little sourly. After all, it had been his date.

The girl never did see the ghost, but she was fond of Henri, and it was five months before the cramped cabin and the lack of a toilet drove her out.

CHAPTER XXIII

A BLACK gloom settled over the Palace Flophouse. All the joy went out of it. Mack came back from the laboratory with his mouth torn and his teeth broken. As a kind of penance, he did not wash his face. He went to his bed and pulled his blanket over his head and he didn't get up all day. His heart was as bruised as his mouth. He went over all the bad things he had done in his life and everything he had ever done seemed bad. He was very sad.

Hughie and Jones sat for a while staring into space and then morosely they went over to the Hediondo Cannery and applied for jobs and got them.

Hazel felt so bad that he walked to Monterey and picked a fight with a soldier and lost it on purpose. That made him feel a little better to be utterly beaten by a man Hazel could have licked without half trying.

Darling was the only happy one of the whole club. She spent the day under Mack's bed happily eating up his shoes. She was a clever dog and her teeth were very sharp. Twice in his black despair, Mack reached under the bed and caught her and put her in bed with him for company, but she squirmed out and went back to eating his shoes.

Eddie mooned on down to 'La Ida' and talked to his friend the bar-tender. He got a few drinks and borrowed some nickels with which he played *Melancholy Baby* five times on the musical-box.

Mack and the boys were under a cloud and they knew it, and they knew they deserved it. They had become social outcasts. All their good intentions were forgotten now. The fact that the party was given for Doc, if it was known, was never mentioned or taken into consideration. The story ran through the Bear Flag. It was told in the canneries. At 'La Ida' drunks discussed it virtuously. Lee Chong refused to comment. He was feeling financially bruised. And the story as it grew went this way: They had stolen liquor and money. They had maliciously broken into the laboratory and systematically destroyed it out of pure malice and evil. People who really knew better took this view. Some of the drunks at 'La Ida' considered going over and beating the hell out of the whole lot of them to show them they couldn't do a thing like that to Doc.

Only a sense of the solidarity and fighting ability of Mack and the boys saved them from some kind of reprisal. There were people who felt virtuous about the affair who hadn't had the material of virtue for a long time. The fiercest of the whole lot was Tom Sheligan, who would have been at the party if he had known about it.

Socially Mack and the boys were beyond the pale. Sam Malloy didn't speak to them as they went by the boiler. They drew into themselves and no one could foresee how they would come out of the cloud. For there are two possible reactions to social ostracism – either a man emerges determined to be better, purer, and kindlier or he goes bad, challenges the world, and does even worse things. This last is by far the commonest reaction to stigma.

Mack and the boys balanced on the scales of good and evil. They were kind and sweet to Darling: they were forbearing and patient with one another. When the first reaction was over they gave the Palace Flophouse a cleaning such as it had never had. They polished the bright work on the stove and they washed all their clothes and blankets. Financially they had become dull and solvent. Hughie and

Jones were working and bringing home their pay. They bought groceries up the hill at the Thrift Market because they could not stand the reproving eyes of Lee Chong.

It was during this time that Doc made an observation which may have been true, but since there was one factor missing in his reasoning it is not known whether he was correct. It was the Fourth of July. Doc was sitting in the laboratory with Richard Frost. They drank beer and listened to a new album of Scarlatti and looked out the window. In front of the Palace Flophouse there was a large log of wood where Mack and the boys were sitting in the mid-morning sun. They faced down the hill toward the laboratory.

Doc said: 'Look at them. There are your true philosophers. I think,' he went on, 'that Mack and the boys know everything that has ever happened in the world and possibly everything that will happen. I think they survive in this particular world better than other people. In a time when people tear themselves to pieces with ambition and nervousness and covetousness, they are relaxed. All of our so-called successful men are sick men, with bad stomachs, and bad souls, but Mack and the boys are healthy and curiously clean. They can do what they want. They can satisfy their appetites without calling them something else.' This speech so dried out Doc's throat that he drained his beer glass. He waved two fingers in the air and smiled. 'There's nothing like that first taste of beer,' he said.

Richard Frost said: 'I think they're just like anyone else. They just haven't any money.'

'They could get it,' Doc said. 'They could ruin their lives and get money. Mack has qualities of genius. They're all very clever if they want something. They just know the nature of things too well to be caught in that wanting.'

If Doc had known of the sadness of Mack and the boys he would not have made the next statement, but no one had told him about the social pressure that was exerted against the inmates of the Palace.

He poured beer slowly into his glass. 'I think I can show you proof,' he said. 'You see how they are sitting facing this way? Well – in about half an hour the Fourth of July Parade is going to pass on Lighthouse Avenue. By just turning their heads they can see it, by standing up they can watch it, and by walking two short blocks they can be right beside it. Now I'll bet you a quart of beer they won't even turn their heads.'

'Suppose they don't?' said Richard Frost. 'What will that prove?'

'What will it prove?' cried Doc. 'Why, just that they know what will be in the parade. They will know that the Mayor will ride first in an automobile with bunting streaming back from the hood. Next will come Long Bob on his white horse with the flag. Then the city council, then two companies of soldiers from the Presidio, next the Elks with purple umbrellas, then the Knights Templars in white ostrich feathers and carrying swords. Next the Knights of Columbus with red ostrich feathers and carrying swords. Mack and the boys know that. The band will play. They've seen it all. They don't have to look again.'

'The man doesn't live who doesn't have to look at a parade,' said Richard Frost.

'Is it a bet then?'

'It's a bet.'

'It has always seemed strange to me,' said Doc. 'The things we admire in men, kindness and generosity, openness, honesty, understanding, and feeling are the concomitants of failure in our system. And those traits we detest, sharpness, greed, acquisitiveness, meanness, egotism, and self-interest are the traits of success. And while men admire the quality of the first they love the produce of the second.'

'Who wants to be good if he has to be hungry too?' said Richard Frost.

'Oh, it isn't a matter of hunger. It's something quite different. The sale of souls to gain the whole world is completely voluntary and almost unanimous – but not quite.

Everywhere in the world there are Mack and the boys. I've seen them in an ice-cream seller in Mexico and in an Aleut in Alaska. You know how they tried to give me a party and something went wrong. But they wanted to give me a party. That was their impulse. Listen,' said Doc. 'Isn't that the band I hear?' Quickly he filled two glasses with beer and the two of them stepped close to the window.

Mack and the boys sat dejectedly on their log and faced the laboratory. The sound of the band came from Lighthouse Avenue, the drums echoing back from the buildings. And suddenly the Mayor's car crossed and it sprayed bunting from the radiator – then Long Bob on his white horse carrying the flag, then the band, then the soldiers, the Elks, the Knights Templar, the Knights of Columbus. Richard and the Doc leaned forward tensely, but they were watching the line of men sitting on the log.

And not a head turned, not a neck straightened up. The parade filed past and they did not move. And the parade was gone. Doc drained his glass and waved two fingers gently in the air and he said: 'Hah! There's nothing in the world like that first taste of beer.'

Richard started for the door. 'What kind of beer do you want?'

'The same kind,' said Doc gently. He was smiling up the hill at Mack and the boys.

It's all fine to say: 'Time will heal everything, this too shall pass away. People will forget' – and things like that when you are not involved, but when you are there is no passage of time, people do not forget, and you are in the middle of something that does not change. Doc didn't know the pain and self-destructive criticism in the Palace Flophouse or he might have tried to do something about it. And Mack and the boys did not know how he felt or they would have held up their heads again.

It was a bad time. Evil stalked darkly in the vacant lot. Sam Malloy had a number of fights with his wife and she cried all the time. The echoes inside the boiler made it sound as though she were crying under water. Mack and the boys seemed to be the node of trouble. The nice bouncer at the Bear Flag threw out a drunk, but threw him too hard and too far and broke his back. Alfred had to go over to Salinas three times before it was cleared up, and that didn't make Alfred feel very well. Ordinarily he was too good a bouncer to hurt anyone. His A and C was a miracle of rhythm and grace.

On top of that a group of high-minded ladies in the town demanded that the dens of vice must close to protect young American manhood. This happened about once a year in the dead period between the Fourth of July and the County Fair. Dora usually closed the Bear Flag for a week when it happened. It wasn't so bad. Everyone got a vacation and little repairs to the plumbing and the walls could be made. But this year the ladies went on a real crusade. They wanted somebody's scalp. It had been a dull summer and they were restless. It got so bad that they had to be told who actually owned the property where vice was practised, what the rents were, and what little hardships might be the result of their closing. That was how close they were to being a serious menace.

Dora was closed a full two weeks and there were three conventions in Monterey while the Bear Flag was closed. Word got around and Monterey lost five conventions for the following year. Things were bad all over. Doc had to get a loan at the bank to pay for the glass that was broken at the party. Elmer Rechati went to sleep on the Southern Pacific track and lost both legs. A sudden and completely unexpected storm tore a purse-seiner and three lampara boats loose from their moorings and tossed them broken and sad on Del Monte beach.

There is no explaining a series of misfortunes like that. Every man blames himself. People in their black minds remember sins committed secretly and wonder whether they have caused the evil sequence. One man may put it down to sun-spots while another invoking the law of probabilities doesn't believe it. Not even the doctors had a good time of it, for while many people were sick none of it was good-paying sickness. It was nothing a good physic or a patent medicine wouldn't take care of.

And to cap it all, Darling got sick. She was a very fat and lively puppy when she was struck down, but five days of fever reduced her to a little skin-covered skeleton. Her liver-coloured nose was pink and her gums were white. Her eyes glazed with illness and her whole body was hot, although she trembled sometimes with cold. She wouldn't eat and she wouldn't drink and her fat little belly shrivelled up against her spine, and even her tail showed the articulations through the skin. It was obviously distemper.

Now a genuine panic came over the Palace Flophouse. Darling had come to be vastly important to them. Hughie and Jones instantly quit their jobs so they could be near to help. They sat up in shifts. They kept a cool, damp cloth on her forehead and she got weaker and weaker. Finally, although they didn't want to, Hazel and Jones were chosen to call on Doc. They found him working over a tide-chart while he ate a chicken stew of which the principal ingredient was not chicken but sea cucumber. They thought he looked at them a little coldly.

'It's Darling,' they said. 'She's sick.'

'What's the matter with her?'

'Mack says it's distemper.'

'I'm no veterinarian,' said Doc. 'I don't know how to treat these things.'

Hazel said: 'Well, couldn't you just take a look at her? She's sick as hell.'

They stood in a circle while Doc examined Darling. He looked at her eyeballs and her gums and felt in her ear for fever. He ran his finger over the ribs that stuck out like spokes and at the poor spine. 'She won't eat?' he asked.

'Not a thing,' said Mack.

'You'll have to force feed her – strong soups and eggs and cod liver oil.'

They thought he was cold and professional. He went back to his tide-charts and his stew.

But Mack and the boys had something to do now. They boiled meat until it was as strong as whisky. They put cod liver oil far back on her tongue so that some of it got down her. They held up her head and made a little funnel of her chops and poured the cool soup in. She had to swallow or drown. Every two hours they fed her and gave her water. Before they had slept in shifts – now no one slept. They sat silently and waited for Darling's crisis.

It came early in the morning. The boys sat in their chairs half asleep, but Mack was awake and his eyes were on the puppy. He saw her ears flip twice, and her chest heave. With infinite weakness she climbed slowly to her spindly legs, dragged herself to the door, took four laps of water, and collapsed on the floor.

Mack shouted the others awake. He danced heavily. All the boys shouted at one another. Lee Chong heard them and snorted to himself as he carried out the garbage cans. Alfred the bouncer heard them and thought they were having a party.

By nine o'clock Darling had eaten a raw egg and half a pint of whipped cream by herself. By noon she was visibly putting on weight. In a day she romped a little and by the end of the week she was a well dog.

At last a crack had developed in the wall of evil. There were evidences of it everywhere. The purse-seiner was hauled back into the water and floated. Word came down to Dora that it was all right to open up the Bear Flag. Earl Wakefield caught a sculpin with two heads and sold it to the museum for eight dollars. The wall of evil and of waiting was broken. It broke away in chinks. The curtains were drawn at the laboratory that night and the Gregorian music played until two o'clock and then the music stopped and no one came out. Some force wrought with Lee Chong's heart and all in an Oriental moment he forgave Mack and the boys and wrote off the frog debt, which had been a monetary headache from the beginning. And to prove to the boys that he had forgiven them he took a pint of Old Tennis Shoes up and presented it to them. Their trading at the Thrift Market had hurt his feelings, but it was all over now. Lee's visit coincided with the first destructive healthy impulse Darling had since her illness. She was completely spoiled now and no one thought of housebreaking her. When Lee Chong came in with his gift, Darling was deliberately and happily destroying Hazel's only pair of rubber-boots, while her happy masters applauded her.

Mack never visited the Bear Flag professionally. It would have seemed a little like incest to him. There was a house out by the baseball park he patronized. Thus, when he went into the front bar, everyone thought he wanted a beer. He stepped up to Alfred. 'Dora around?' he asked.

'What do you want with her?' Alfred asked.

'I got something I want to ask her.'

'What about?'

'That's none of your God damn business,' said Mack.

'Okay. Have it your way. I'll see if she wants to talk to you.'

A moment later he led Mack into the sanctum. Dora sat at a roll-top desk. Her orange hair was piled in ringlets on her head and she wore a green eyeshade. With a stub pen she was bringing her books up-to-date, a fine old double-entry ledger. She was dressed in a magnificent pink silk wrapper with lace at the wrists and throat. When Mack came in she whirled her pivot-chair about and faced him. Alfred stood in the door and waited. Mack stood until Alfred closed the door and left.

Dora scrutinized him suspiciously. 'Well – what can I do for you?' she demanded at last

'You see, ma'am,' said Mack. 'Well I guess you heard what we done over at Doc's some time back.'

Dora pushed the eyeshade back up on her head and she put the pen in an old-fashioned coil-spring holder. 'Yeah!' she said. 'I heard.'

'Well, ma'am, we did it for Doc. You may not believe it but we wanted to give him a party. Only he didn't get home in time and – well, she got out of hand.'

'So I heard,' said Dora. 'Well, what you want me to do?'

'Well,' said Mack, 'I and the boys thought we'd ask you. You know what we think of Doc. We wanted to ask you what you thought we could do for him that would kind of show him.'

Dora said: 'Hum,' and she flopped back in her pivot-chair and crossed her legs and smoothed her wrapper over her knees. She shook out a cigarette, lighted it, and studied. 'You gave him a party he didn't get to. Why don't you give him a party he does get to?' she said.

'Jesus,' said Mack afterwards talking to the boys. 'It was just as simple as that. Now there is one hell of a woman. No wonder she got to be madam. There is one hell of a woman.'

CHAPTER XXIV

MARY TALBOT, Mrs Tom Talbot, that is, was lovely. She had red hair with green lights in it. Her skin was golden, with a green under-cast, and her eyes were green, with little golden spots. Her face was triangular, with wide cheek-bones, wide-set eyes, and her chin was pointed. She had long dancer's legs and dancer's feet, and she seemed never to touch the ground when she walked. When she was excited, and she was excited a good deal of the time, her face flushed with gold. Her great-great-great-great-great grandmother had been burned as a witch.

More than anything in the world Mary Talbot loved parties. She loved to give parties and she loved to go to parties. Since Tom Talbot didn't make much money Mary couldn't give parties all the time, so she tricked people into giving them. Sometimes she telephoned a friend and said bluntly: 'Isn't it about time you gave a party?'

Regularly, Mary had six birthdays a year, and she organized costume parties, surprise parties, holiday parties. Christmas Eve at her house was a very exciting thing. For Mary glowed with parties. She carried her husband along on the wave of her excitement.

In the afternoons when Tom was at work Mary sometimes gave tea-parties for the neighbourhood cats. She set a footstool with doll cups and saucers. She gathered the cats, and there were plenty of them, and then she held long and detailed conversations with them. It was a kind of play she enjoyed very much – a kind of satiric game, and it covered and concealed from Mary the fact that she didn't have very nice clothes and the Talbots didn't have any money. They were pretty near absolute bottom most of the time, and when they really scraped, Mary managed to give some kind of a party.

She could do that. She could infect a whole house with gaiety and she used her gift as a weapon against the despondency that lurked always around outside the house waiting to get in at Tom. That was Mary's job as she saw it – to keep the despondency away from Tom because everyone knew he was going to be a great success some time. Mostly she was successful in keeping the dark things out of the house, but sometimes they got in at Tom and laid him out. Then he would sit and brood for hours, while Mary frantically built up a back-fire of gaiety.

One time when it was the first of the month and there

were curt notes from the water company and the rent wasn't paid and a manuscript had come back from *Collier's* and the cartoons had come back from *The New Yorker* and pleurisy was hurting Tom pretty badly, he went into the bedroom and lay down on the bed.

Mary came softly in, for the blue-grey colour of his gloom had seeped out under the door and through the keyhole. She had a little bouquet of candytuft in a collar of paper lace.

'Smell,' she said and held the bouquet to his nose. He smelled the flowers and said nothing. 'Do you know what day this is?' she asked and thought wildly for something to make it a bright day.

Tom said: 'Why don't we face it for once? We're down. We're going under. What's the good kidding ourselves?'

'No we're not,' said Mary. 'We're magic people. We always have been. Remember that ten dollars you found in a book – remember when your cousin sent you five dollars? Nothing can happen to us.'

'Well, it has happened,' said Tom. 'I'm sorry,' he said. 'I just can't talk myself out of it this time. I'm sick of pretending everything. For once I'd like to have it real – just for once.'

'I thought of giving a little party tonight,' said Mary.

'On what? You're not going to cut out the baked ham picture from a magazine again and serve it on a platter, are you? I'm sick of that kind of kidding. It isn't funny any more. It's sad.'

'I could give a little party,' she insisted. 'Just a small affair. Nobody will dress. It's the anniversary of the founding of the Bloomer League – you didn't even remember that.'

'It's no use,' said Tom. 'I know it's mean, but I just can't rise to it. Why don't you just go out and shut the door and leave me alone? I'll get you down if you don't.'

She looked at him closely and saw that he meant it. Mary walked quietly out and shut the door, and Tom turned over on the bed and put his face down between his arms. He could hear her rustling about in the other room.

She decorated the door with old Christmas things, glass-balls, and tinsel, and she made a placard that said: 'Welcome Tom, our Hero'. She listened at the door and she couldn't hear anything. A little disconsolately she got out the footstool and spread a napkin over it. She put her bouquet in a glass in the middle of the footstool and set out four little cups and saucers. She went into the kitchen, put the tea in the teapot and set the kettle to boil. Then she went out into the yard.

Kitty Randolph was sunning herself by the front fence. Mary said: 'Miss Randolph – I'm having a few friends in to tea if you would care to come.' Kitty Randolph rolled over languorously on her back and stretched in the warm sun. 'Don't be later than four o'clock,' said Mary. 'My husband and I are going to the Bloomer League Centennial Reception at the Hotel.'

She strolled round the house to the backyard, where the blackberry vines clambered over the fence. Kitty Casini was squatting on the ground growling to herself and flicking her tail fiercely. 'Mrs Casini,' Mary began, and then she stopped for she saw what the cat was doing. Kitty Casini had a mouse. She patted it gently with her unarmed paw and the mouse squirmed horribly away, dragging its paralysed hind legs behind it. The cat let it get nearly to the covert of the blackberry vines and then she reached delicately out and white thorns had sprouted on her paw. Daintily she stabbed the mouse through the back and drew it wriggling to her and her tail flicked with tense delight.

Tom must have been at least half asleep when he heard his name called over and over. He jumped up shouting: 'What is it? Where are you?' He could hear Mary crying. He ran out into the yard and saw what was happening. 'Turn your head,' he shouted and he killed the mouse. Kitty Casini had leaped to the top of the fence, where she watched him angrily. Tom picked up a rock and hit her in the stomach and knocked her off the fence.

In the house Mary was still crying a little. She poured the water into the teapot and brought it to the table. 'Sit there,' she told Tom and he squatted down on the floor in front of the footstool.

'Can't I have a big cup?' he asked.

'I can't blame Kitty Casini,' said Mary. 'I know how cats are. It isn't her fault. But – Oh, Tom! I'm going to have trouble inviting her again. I'm just not going to like her for a while no matter how much I want to.' She looked closely at Tom and saw that the lines were gone from his forehead and that he was not blinking badly. 'But then I'm so busy with the Bloomer League these days,' she said. 'I just don't know how I'm going to get everything done.'

Mary Talbot gave a pregnancy party that year. And everyone said: 'God! A kid of hers is going to have fun.'

CHAPTER XXV

CERTAINLY all of Cannery Row and probably all of Monterey felt that a change had come. It's all right not to believe in luck and omens. Nobody believes in them. But it doesn't do any good to take chances with them and no one takes chances. Cannery Row, like every other place else, is not superstitious, but will not walk under a ladder or open an umbrella in the house. Doc was a pure scientist and incapable of superstition and yet when he came in late one night and found a line of white flowers across the door-sill he had a bad time of it. But most people in Cannery Row simply do not believe in such things and then live by them.

There was no doubt in Mack's mind that a dark cloud

had hung on the Palace Flophouse. He had analysed the abortive party and found that a misfortune had crept into every crevice, that bad luck had come up like hives on the evening. And once you got into a routine like that the best thing to do was just go to bed until it was over. You couldn't buck it. Not that Mack was superstitious.

Now a kind of gladness began to penetrate into the Row and to spread out from there. Doc was almost supernaturally successful with a series of lady visitors. He didn't half try. The puppy at the Palace was growing like a pole bean, and, having a thousand generations of training behind her, she began to train herself. She got disgusted with wetting on the floor and took to going outside. It was obvious that Darling was going to grow up a good and charming dog. And she had developed no chorea from her distemper.

The benignant influence crept like gas through the Row. It got as far as Herman's hamburger stand, it spread to the San Carlos Hotel. Jimmy Brucia felt it and Johnny his singing bar-tender. Sparky Evea felt it and joyously joined battle with three new out-of-town cops. It even got as far as the County Jail in Salinas, where Gay, who had lived a good life by letting the sheriff beat him at draughts, suddenly grew cocky and never lost another game. He lost his privileges that way, but he felt a whole man again.

The sea-lions felt it and their barking took on a tone and a cadence that would have gladdened the heart of St Francis. Little girls studying their catechism suddenly looked up and giggled for no reason at all. Perhaps some electrical finder could have been developed so delicate that it could have located the source of all this spreading joy and fortune. And triangulation might possibly have located it in the Palace Flophouse and Grill. Certainly the Palace was lousy with it. Mack and the boys were charged. Jones was seen to leap from his chair only to do a quick tap dance and sit down again. Hazel smiled vaguely at nothing at all. The joy was so general and so suffused that Mack had a hard time keeping it centred and aimed at its objective. Eddie, who had worked at 'La Ida' pretty regularly was accumulating a cellar of some promise. He no longer added beer to the wining jug. It gave a flat taste to the mixture, he said.

Sam Malloy had planted morning glories to grow over the boiler. He had put out a little awning and under it he and his wife often sat in the evening. She was crocheting a bedspread.

The joy even got into the Bear Flag. Business was good. Phyllis Mae's leg was knitting nicely and she was nearly ready to go to work again. Eva Flanagan got back from East St Louis very glad to be back. It had been hot in East St Louis and it hadn't been as fine as she remembered it. But then she had been younger when she had had so much fun there.

The knowledge or conviction about the party for Doc was no sudden thing. It did not burst out full blown. People knew about it, but let it grow gradually, like a pupa in the cocoons of their imaginations.

Mack was realistic about it. 'Last time we forced her,' he told the boys. 'You can't never give a good party that way. You got to let her creep up on you.'

'Well, when's it going to be?' Jones asked impatiently.

'I don't know,' said Mack.

'Is it gonna be a surprise party?' Hazel asked.

'It ought to, that's the best kind,' said Mack.

Darling brought him a tennis ball she had found and he threw it out the door into the weeds. She bounced away after it.

Hazel said: 'If we knew when was Doc's birthday, we could give him a birthday-party.'

Mack's mouth was open. Hazel constantly surprised him. 'By God, Hazel, you got something,' he cried. 'Yes, sir, if it was his birthday there'd be presents. That's just the thing. All we got to find out is when it is.'

'That ought to be easy,' said Hughie. 'Why don't we ask him?'

'Hell,' said Mack. 'Then he'd catch on. You ask a guy when is his birthday and especially if you've already give him a party like we done, and he'll know what you want to know for. Maybe I'll just go over and smell around a little and not let on.'

'I'll go with you,' said Hazel.

'No – if two of us went, he might figure we were up to something.'

'Well, hell, it was my idear,' said Hazel.

'I know,' said Mack. 'And when it comes off why I'll tell Doc it was your idear. But I think I better go over alone.'

'How is he – friendly?' Eddie asked.

'Sure, he's all right.'

Mack found Doc way back in the downstairs part of the laboratory. He was dressed in a long rubber apron and he wore rubber gloves to protect his hands from the formaldehyde. He was injecting the veins and arteries of small dogfish with colour mass. His little ball mill rolled over and over, mixing the blue mass. The red fluid was already in the pressure-gun. Doc's fine hands worked precisely, slipping the needle into place and pressing the compressed-air trigger that forced the colour into the veins. He laid the finished fish in a neat pile. He would have to go over these again to put the blue mass in the arteries. The dog-fish made good dissection specimens.

'Hi, Doc,' said Mack. 'Keepin' pretty busy?'

'Busy as I want,' said Doc. 'How's the pup?'

'Doin' just fine. She would of died if it hadn't been for you.'

For a moment a wave of caution went over Doc and then slipped off. Ordinarily a compliment made him wary. He had been dealing with Mack for a long time. But the tone had nothing but gratefulness in it. He knew how Mack felt about the pup. 'How are things going up at the Palace?'

'Fine, Doc, just fine. We got two new chairs. I wish you'd come up and see us. It's pretty nice up there now.'

'I will,' said Doc. 'Eddie still bring back the jug?'

'Sure,' said Mack. 'He ain't puttin' beer in it no more and I think the stuff is better. It's got more zip.'

'It had plenty of zip before,' said Doc.

Mack waited patiently. Sooner or later Doc was going to wade into it and he was waiting. If Doc seemed to open the subject himself it would be less suspicious. This was always Mack's method.

'Haven't seen Hazel for some time. He isn't sick, is he?'

'No,' said Mack and he opened the campaign. 'Hazel is all right. Him and Hughie are havin' one hell of a battle. Been goin' on for a week,' he chuckled. 'An' the funny thing is it's about somethin' they don't neither of them know nothin' about. I stayed out of it because I don't know nothin' about it neither, but not them. They've even got a little mad at each other.'

'What's it about?' Doc asked.

'Well, sir,' said Mack, 'Hazel's all the time buyin' these here charts and lookin' up lucky days and stars and stuff like that. And Hughie says it's all a bunch of malarky. Hazel, he says if you know when a guy is born you can tell about him and Hughie says they're just sellin' Hazel them charts for two bits apiece. Me, I don't know nothin' about it. What do you think, Doc?'

'I'd kind of side with Hughie,' said Doc. He stopped the ball mill, washed out the colour-gun and filled it with blue mass.

'They got goin' hot the other night,' said Mack. 'They ask me when I'm born so I tell 'em April 12 and Hazel he goes and buys one of them charts and read all about me. Well it did seem to hit in some places. But it was nearly all good stuff and a guy will believe good stuff about himself. It said I'm brave and smart and kind to my friends. But Hazel says it's all true. When's your birthday, Doc?' At the end of the long discussion it sounded perfectly casual. You couldn't put your finger on it. But it must be remembered that Doc had known Mack a very long time. If he had not he would have said December 18, which was his birthday, instead of October 27, which was not. 'October 27,' said Doc. 'Ask Hazel what that makes me.'

'It's probably so much malarky,' said Mack, 'but Hazel he takes it serious. I'll ask him to look you up, Doc.'

When Mack left, Doc wondered casually what the build-up was. For he had recognized it as a lead. He knew Mack's technique, his method. He recognized his style. And he wondered to what purpose Mack could put the information. It was only later, when rumours began to creep in, that Doc added the whole thing up. Now he felt slightly relieved, for he had expected Mack to put the bite on him.

CHAPTER XXVI

THE two little boys played in the boat works yard until a cat climbed the fence. Instantly they gave chase, drove it across the tracks, and there filled their pockets with granite stones from the roadbed. The cat got away from them in the tall weeds, but they kept the stones because they were perfect in weight, shape, and size for throwing. You can't ever tell when you're going to need a stone like that. They turned down Cannery Row and whanged a stone at the cor-rugated-iron front of Morden's Cannery. A startled man looked out the office window and then rushed for the door, but the boys were too quick for him. They were lying behind a wooden stringer in the lot before he even got near the door. He couldn't have found them in a hundred years.

'I bet he could look all his life and he couldn't find us,' said Joey.

They got tired of hiding after a while with no one looking for them. They got up and strolled on down Cannery Row. They looked a long time in Lee's window, coveting the pliers, the hacksaws, the engineers' caps, and the bananas. Then they crossed the street and sat down on the lower step of the stairs that went to the second storey of the laboratory.

Joey said: 'You know, this guy in here got babies in bottles.'

'What kind of babies?' Willard asked.

'Regular babies, only before they're borned.'

'I don't believe it,' said Willard.

'Well, it's true. The Sprague kid seen them and he says they ain't no bigger than this and they got little hands and feet and eyes.'

'And hair?' Willard demanded.

'Well, the Sprague kid didn't say about hair.'

'You should of asked him. I think he's a liar.'

'You better not let him hear you say that,' said Joey.

'Well, you can tell him I said it. I ain't afraid of him and I ain't afraid of you. I ain't afraid of anybody. You want to make something of it?' Joey didn't answer. 'Well, do you?'

'No,' said Joey. 'I was thinkin', why don't we just go up and ask the guy if he's got babies in bottles? Maybe he'd show them to us, that is if he's got any.'

'He ain't there,' said Willard. 'When he's here, his car's here. He's away some place. I think it's a lie. I think the Sprague kid is a liar. I think you're a liar. You want to make something of that?'

It was a lazy day. Willard was going to have to work hard to get up any excitement. 'I think you're a coward too. You want to make something of that?' Joey didn't answer. Willard changed his tactics. 'Where's your old man now?' he asked in a conversational tone.

'He's dead,' said Joey.

'Oh yeah? I didn't hear. What'd he die of?'

For a moment Joey was silent. He knew Willard knew, but he couldn't let on he knew, not without fighting Willard, and Joey was afraid of Willard.

'He committed – he killed himself.'

'Yeah?' Willard put on a long face. 'How'd he do it?'

'He took rat poison.'

Willard's voice shrieked with laughter. 'What'd he think he was – a rat?'

Joey chuckled a little at the joke, just enough, that is.

'He must of thought he was a rat,' Willard cried. 'Did he go crawling around like this – look Joey – like this? Did he wrinkle up his nose like this? Did he have a big old long tail?' Willard was helpless with laughter. 'Why'n't he just get a rat-trap and put his head in it?' They laughed themselves out on that one. Willard really wore it out. Then he probed for another joke. 'What'd he look like when he took it – like this?' He crossed his eyes and opened his mouth and stuck out his tongue.

'He was sick all day,' said Joey. 'He didn't die 'til the middle of the night. It hurt him.'

Willard said: 'What'd he do it for?'

'He couldn't get a job,' said Joey. 'Nearly a year he couldn't get a job. And you know a funny thing? The next morning a guy come around to give him a job.'

Willard tried to recapture his joke. 'I guess he just figured he was a rat,' he said, but it fell through even for Willard.

Joey stood up and put his hands in his pockets. He saw a little coppery shine in the gutter and walked toward it, but just as he reached it Willard shoved him aside and picked up the penny.

'I saw it first,' Joey cried. 'It's mine.'

'You want to try and make something of it?' said Willard. 'Why'n't you go and take rat poison?'

CHAPTER XXVII

MACK and the boys – the Virtues, the Beatitudes, the Beauties. They sat in the Palace Flophouse and they were the stone dropped in the pool, the impulse which sent out ripples to all of Cannery Row and beyond, to Pacific Grove, to Monterey, even over the hill to Carmel.

'This time,' said Mack, 'we got to be sure he gets to the party. If he don't get there, we don't give it.'

'Where we going to give it this time?' Jones asked.

Mack tipped his chair back against the wall and hooked his feet around the front legs. 'I've give that a lot of thought,' he said. 'Of course we could give it here, but it would be pretty hard to surprise him here. And Doc likes his own place. He's got his music there.' Mack scowled around the room. 'I don't know who broke his phonograph last time,' he said. 'But if anybody so much as lays a finger on it next time I personally will kick the hell out of him.'

'I guess we'll just have to give it at his place,' said Hughie.

People didn't get the news of the party – the knowledge of it just slowly grew up in them. And no one was invited. Everyone was going. October 27 had a mental red circle around it. And since it was to be a birthday party there were presents to be considered.

Take the girls at Dora's. All of them had at one time or another gone over to the laboratory for advice or medicine or simply for unprofessional company. And they had seen Doc's bed. It was covered with an old faded red blanket full of fox tails and burrs and sand, for he took it on all his collecting trips. If money came in he bought laboratory equipment. It never occurred to him to buy a new blanket for himself. Dora's girls were making a patchwork quilt, a beautiful thing of silk. And since most of the silks available came from underclothing and evening dresses, the quilt was glorious in strips of flesh pink and orchid and pale-yellow and cerise. They worked on it in the late mornings and in the afternoons before the boys from the sardine fleet came in. Under the community of effort, those fights and ill feelings that always are present in a whore-house completely disappeared.

Lee Chong got out and inspected a twenty-five-foot string of fire-crackers and a big bag of China lily bulbs. These to his way of thinking were the finest things you could have for a party.

Sam Malloy had long had a theory of antiques. He knew that old furniture and glass and crockery, which had not been very valuable in its day, had when time went by taken on desirability and cash value out of all proportion to its beauty or utility. He knew of one chair that had brought five hundred dollars. Sam collected pieces of historic automobiles and he was convinced that some day his collection, after making him very rich, would repose on black velvet in the best museums. Sam gave the party a good deal of thought and then he went over his treasures, which he kept in a big locked box behind the boiler. He decided to give Doc one of his finest pieces – the connecting-rod and piston from a 1916 Chalmers. He rubbed and polished this beauty until it gleamed like a piece of ancient armour. He made a little box for it and lined it with black cloth.

Mack and the boys gave the problem considerable thought and came to the conclusion that Doc always wanted cats and had some trouble getting them. Mack brought out his double cage. They borrowed a female in an interesting condition and set their trap under the cypress-tree at the top of the vacant lot. In the corner of the Palace they built a wire cage and in it their collection of angry tom-cats grew every night. Jones had to make two trips a day to the canneries for fish heads to feed their charges. Mack considered correctly that twenty-five tom-cats would be as nice a present as they could give Doc.

'No decorations this time,' said Mack. 'Just a good solid party with lots of liquor.'

Gay heard about the party clear over in the Salinas jail, and he made a deal with the sheriff to get off that night, and borrowed two dollars from him for a round-trip bus ticket. Gay had been very nice to the sheriff, who wasn't a man to forget it, particularly because election was coming up and Gay could, or said he could, swing quite a few votes. Besides, Gay could give the Salinas jail a bad name if he wanted to.

Henri had suddenly decided that the old-fashioned pin-cushion was an art form which had flowered and reached its peak in the 'Nineties and had since been neglected. He revived the form and was delighted to see what could be done with coloured pins. The picture was never completed – you could change it by re-arranging the pins. He was preparing a group of these pieces for a one-man show when he heard about the party, and he finally abandoned his own work and began a giant pin-cushion for Doc. It was to be an intricate and provocative design in green, yellow, and blue pins, all cool colours, and its title was Pre-Cambrian Memory.

Henri's friend Eric, a learned barber who collected the first editions of writers who never had a second edition or a second book, decided to give Doc a rowing-machine he had got at the bankruptcy proceedings of a client with a three-year barber bill. The rowing-machine was in fine condition. No one had rowed it much. No one ever uses a rowing-machine.

The conspiracy grew and there were endless visits back and forth, discussions of presents, of liquor, of what time will we start and nobody must tell Doc.

Doc didn't know when he first became aware that something was going on that concerned him. In Lee Chong's, conversation stopped when he entered. At first it seemed to him that people were cold to him. When at least half a dozen people asked him what he was doing October 27 he was puzzled, for he had forgotten he had given this date as his birthday. Actually he had been interested in the horoscope for a spurious birthdate, but Mack had never mentioned it again and so Doc forgot it.

One evening he stopped in at the Halfway House because they had a draught beer he liked and kept it at the right temperature. He gulped his first glass and then settled down to enjoy his second when he heard a drunk talking to the bar-tender. 'You goin' to the party?'

'What party?'

'Well,' said the drunk confidentially, 'you know Doc, down in Cannery Row.'

The bar-tender looked up the bar and then back.

'Well,' said the drunk, 'they're givin' him a hell of a party on his birthday.'

'Who is?'

'Everybody.'

Doc mulled this over. He did not know the drunk at all.

His reaction to the idea was not simple. He felt a great warmth that they should want to give him a party and at the same time he quaked inwardly, remembering the last one they had given.

Now everything fell into place – Mack's question and the silences when he was about. He thought of it a lot that night sitting beside his desk. He glanced about, considering what things would have to be locked up. He knew the party was going to cost him plenty.

The next day he began making his own preparations for the party. His best records he carried into the back room, where they could be locked away. He moved every bit of equipment that was breakable back there too. He knew how ıt would be – his guests would be hungry and they wouldn't bring anything to eat. They would run out of liquor early, they always did. A little wearily he went up to the Thrift Market, where there was a fine and understanding butcher. They discussed meat for some time. Doc ordered fifteen pounds of steak, ten pounds of tomatoes, twelve heads of lettuces, six loaves of bread, a big jar of peanut butter, and one of strawberry jam, five gallons of wine, and four quarts of a good substantial, but not distinguished, whisky. He knew he would have trouble at the bank the first of the month. Three or four such parties, he thought, and he would lose the laboratory.

Meanwhile, on the Row, the planning reached a crescendo. Doc was right, no one thought of food, but there were odd pints and quarts put away all over. The collection of presents was growing and the guest list, if there had been one, was a little like a census. At the Bear Flag a constant discussion went on about what to wear. Since they would not be working, the girls did not want to wear the long beautiful dresses which were their uniforms. They decided to wear street clothes. It wasn't as simple as it sounded. Dora insisted that a skeleton crew remain on duty to take care of the regulars. The girls divided up into shifts, some to stay until they were relieved by others. They had to flip for who would go to the party first. The first ones would see Doc's face when they gave him the beautiful quilt. They had it on a frame in the dining-room and it was nearly finished. Mrs Malloy had put aside her bedspread for a while. She was crocheting six doilies for Doc's beer glasses. The first excitement was gone from the Row now and its place was taken by a deadly cumulative earnestness. There were fifteen tomcats in the cage at the Palace Flophouse and their yowling made Darling a little nervous at night.

CHAPTER XXVIII

SOONER or later Frankie was bound to hear about the party. For Frankie drifted about like a small cloud. He was always on the edge of groups. No one noticed him or paid any attention to him. You couldn't tell whether he was listening or not. But Frankie did hear about the party and he heard about the presents and a feeling of fullness swelled in him and a feeling of sick longing.

In the window of Jacob's Jewellery Store was the most beautiful thing in the world. It had been there a long time. It was a black onyx clock with a gold face, but on top of it was the real beauty. On top was a bronze group – St George killing the dragon. The dragon was on his back with his claws in the air and in his breast was St George's spear. The Saint was in full armour, with the visor raised, and he rode a fat, big-buttocked horse. With his spear he pinned the dragon to the ground. But the wonderful thing was that he wore a pointed beard and he looked a little like Doc.

Frankie walked to Alvarado Street several times a week to stand in front of the window and look at this beauty. He dreamed about it too, dreamed of running his fingers over the rich, smooth bronze. He had known about it for months when he heard of the party and the presents.

Frankie stood on the pavement for an hour before he went inside. 'Well?' said Mr Jacobs. He had given Frankie a visual searching as he came in and he knew there wasn't seventy-five cents on him.

'How much is that?' Frankie asked huskily.

'What?'

'That.'

'You mean the clock? Fifty dollars – with the group seventy-five dollars.'

Frankie walked out without replying. He went down to the beach and crawled under an overturned rowboat and peeked out at the little waves. The bronze beauty was so strong in his head that it seemed to stand out in front of him. And a frantic trapped feeling came over him. He had to get the beauty. His eyes were fierce when he thought of it.

He stayed under the boat all day and at night he emerged and went back to Alvarado Street. While people went to the movies and came out and went to the Golden Poppy, he walked up and down the block. And he didn't get tired or sleepy, for the beauty burned in him like fire.

At last the people thinned out and gradually disappeared from the streets and the parked cars drove away and the town settled to sleep.

A policeman looked closely at Frankie. 'What you doing out?' he asked.

Frankie took to his heels and fled around the corner and hid behind a barrel in the alley. At two-thirty he crept to the door of Jacob's and tried the knob. It was locked. Frankie went back to the alley and sat behind the barrel and thought. He saw a broken piece of concrete lying beside the barrel and he picked it up.

The policeman reported that he heard the crash and ran to it. Jacob's window was broken. He saw the prisoner walking rapidly away and chased him. He didn't know how the boy could run that far and that fast carrying fifty pounds of clock and bronze, but the prisoner nearly got away. If he had not blundered into a blind street he would have got away.

The chief called Doc the next day. 'Come on down, will you? I want to talk to you.'

They brought Frankie in very dirty and frowzy. His eyes

were red, but he held his mouth firm and he even smiled a little welcome when he saw Doc.

'What's the matter, Frankie?' Doc asked.

'He broke into Jacob's last night,' the chief said. 'Stole some stuff. We got in touch with his mother. She says it's not her fault, because he hangs around your place all the time.'

'Frankie – you shouldn't have done it,' said Doc. The heavy stone of inevitability was on his heart. 'Can't you parole him to me?' Doc asked.

'I don't think the judge will do it,' said the chief. 'We've got a mental report. You know what's wrong with him?'

'Yes,' said Doc. 'I know.'

'And you know what's likely to happen when he comes into puberty?'

'Yes,' said Doc, 'I know,' and the stone weighed terribly on his heart.

'The doctor thinks we better put him away. We couldn't before, but now he's got a felony on him, I think we better.'

As Frankie listened the welcome died in his eyes.

'What did he take?' Doc asked.

'A great big clock and a bronze statue.'

'I'll pay for it.'

'Oh, we got it back. I don't think the judge will hear of it. It'll just happen again. You know that.'

'Yes,' said Doc softly, 'I know. But maybe he had a reason. Frankie,' he said, 'why did you take it?'

Frankie looked a long time at him. 'I love you,' he said.

Doc ran out and got in his car and went collecting in the caves below Pt Lobos.

CHAPTER XXIX

At four o'clock on October 27 Doc finished bottling the last of a lot of jelly-fish. He washed out the formaline jug, cleaned his forceps, powdered and took off his rubber-gloves. He went upstairs, fed the rats, and put some of his best records and his microscopes in the back room. Then he locked it. Sometimes an illuminated guest wanted to play with the rattlesnakes. By making careful preparations, by foreseeing possibilities, Doc hoped to make this party as non-lethal as possible without making it dull.

He put on a pot of coffee, started the *Great Fugue* on the phonograph, and took a shower. He was very quick about it, for he was dressed in clean clothes and was having his cup of coffee before the music was completed.

He looked out through the window at the lot and up at the Palace, but no one was moving. Doc didn't know who or how many were coming to his party. But he knew he was watched. He had been conscious of it all day. Not that he had seen anyone, but someone or several people had kept him in sight. So it was to be a surprise party. He might as well be surprised. He would follow his usual routine, as though nothing were happening. He crossed to Lee Chong's and bought two quarts of beer. There seemed to be a suppressed Oriental excitement at Lee's. So they were coming too. Doc went back to the laboratory and poured out a glass of beer. He drank the first off for thirst and poured a second one to taste. The lot and the street were still deserted.

Mack and the boys were in the Palace and the door was closed. All afternoon the stove had roared, heating water for baths. Even Darling had been bathed and she wore a red bow round her neck.

'What time you think we should go over?' Hazel asked.

'I don't think before eight o'clock,' said Mack. 'But I don't see nothin' against us havin' a short one to kind of get warmed up.'

'How about Doc getting warmed up?' Hughie said. 'Maybe I ought to just take him a bottle like it was just nothing.'

'No,' said Mack. 'Doc just went over to Lee's for some beer.'

'You think he suspects anything?' Jones asked.

'How could he?' asked Mack.

In the corner cage two tom-cats started an argument and the whole cageful commented with growls and arched backs. There were only twenty-one cats. They had fallen short of their mark.

'I wonder how they'll get them cats over there?' Hazel began. 'We can't carry that big cage through the door.'

'We won't,' said Mack. 'Remember how it was with the frogs. No, we'll just tell Doc about them. He can come over and get them.' Mack got up and opened one of Eddie's wining jugs. 'We might as well get warmed up,' he said.

At five-thirty the old Chinaman flap-flapped down the hill, past the Palace. He crossed the lot, crossed the street, and disappeared between Western Biological and the Hediondo.

At the Bear Flag the girls were getting ready. A kind of anchor watch had been chosen by straws. The ones who stayed were to be relieved every hour.

Dora was splendid. Her hair freshly dyed orange was curled and piled on her head. She wore her wedding ring and a big diamond brooch on her breast. Her dress was white silk, with a black bamboo pattern. In the bedrooms the reverse of ordinary procedure was in practice.

Those who were staying wore long evening dresses, while

those who were going had on short print dresses and looked very pretty. The quilt, finished and backed, was in a big cardboard box in the bar. The bouncer grumbled a little, for it had been decided that he couldn't go to the party. Someone had to look after the house. Contrary to orders, each girl had a pint hidden and each girl watched for the signal to fortify herself a little for the party.

Dora strode magnificently into her office and closed the door. She unlocked the top drawer of the roll-top desk, took out a bottle and a glass, and poured herself a snort. And the bottle clinked softly on the glass. A girl listening outside the door heard the clink and spread the word. Dora would not be able to smell breaths now. And the girls rushed for their rooms and got out their pints. Dusk had come to Cannery Row, the grey time between daylight and street light. Phyllis Mae peeked round the curtain in the front parlour.

'Can you see him?' Doris asked.

'Yeah. He's got the lights on. He's sitting there like he's reading. Jesus, how that guy does read. You'd think he'd ruin his eyes. He's got a glass of beer in his hand.'

'Well,' said Doris, 'we might as well have a little one, I guess.'

Phyllis Mae was still limping a little, but she was as good as new. She could, she said, lick her weight in City Councilmen. 'Seems kind of funny,' she said. 'There he is, sitting over there and he don't know what's going to happen.'

'He never comes in here for a trick,' Doris said a little sadly.

'Lots of guys don't want to pay,' said Phyllis Mae. 'Costs them more, but they figure it different.'

'Well, hell, maybe he likes them.'

'Likes who?'

'Them girls that go over there.'

'Oh, yeah – maybe he does. I been over there. He never made a pass at me.'

'He wouldn't,' said Doris. 'But that don't mean if you didn't work here you wouldn't have to fight your way out.'

'You mean he don't like our profession.'

'No, I don't mean that at all. He probably figures a girl that's workin' has got a different attitude.'

They had another small snort.

In her office Dora poured herself one more, swallowed it, and locked the drawer again. She fixed her perfect hair in the wall mirror, inspected her shining red nails, and went out to the bar. Alfred the bouncer was sulking. It wasn't anything he said nor was his expression unpleasant, but he was sulking just the same. Dora looked him over coldly. 'I guess you figure you're getting the blocks, don't you?'

'No,' said Alfred. 'No, it's quite all right.'

That quite threw Dora. 'Quite all right, is it? You got a job, Mister. Do you want to keep it or not?'

'It's quite all right,' Alfred said frostily. 'I ain't putting out no beef.' He put his elbows on the bar and studied himself in the mirror. 'You just go and enjoy yourself,' he said. 'I'll take care of everything here. You don't need to worry.'

Dora melted under his pain. 'Look,' she said. 'I don't like to have the place without a man. Some lush might get smart and the kids couldn't handle him. But a little later you can come over and you could kind of keep your eye on the place out of the window. How would that be? You could see if anything happened.'

'Well,' said Alfred, 'I would like to come.' He was mollified by her permission. 'Later I might drop over for just a minute or two. They was a mean drunk in last night. An' I don't know, Dora – I kind of lost my nerve since I bust that guy's back. I just ain't sure of myself no more. I'm gonna pull a punch some night and get took.'

'You need a rest,' said Dora. 'Maybe I'll get Mack to fill in and you can take a couple of weeks off.' She was a wonderful madam, Dora was.

Over at the laboratory, Doc had a little whisky after his beer. He was feeling a little mellow. It seemed a nice thing to him that they would give him a party. He played the

Pavane to a Dead Princess and felt sentimental and a little sad. And because of his feeling he went on with *Daphnis and Chloe*. There was a passage in it that reminded him of something else. The observers in Athens before Marathon reported seeing a great line of dust crossing the Plain, and they heard the clash of arms and they heard the Eleusinian Chant. There was part of the music that reminded him of that picture.

When it was done he got another whisky and he debated in his mind about the *Brandenburg*. That would snap him out of the sweet and sickly mood he was getting into. But what was wrong with the sweet and sickly mood? It was rather pleasant. 'I can play anything I want,' he said aloud. 'I can play *Clair de Lune* or *The Maiden with Flaxen Hair*. I'm a free man.'

He poured a whisky and drank it. And he compromised with the *Moonlight Sonata*. He could see the neon light of 'La Ida' blinking on and off. And then the street light in front of the Bear Flag came on.

A squadron of huge brown beetles hurled themselves against the light and then fell to the ground and moved their legs and felt around with their antennae. A lady cat strolled lonesomely along the gutter looking for adventure. She wondered what had happened to all the tom-cats who had made life interesting and the nights hideous.

Mr Malloy on his hands and knees peered out of the boiler door to see if anyone had gone to the party yet. In the Palace the boys sat restlessly watching the black hands of the alarm clock.

CHAPTER XXX

THE nature of parties has been imperfectly studied. It is, however, generally understood that a party has a pathology, that it is a kind of an individual, and that it is likely to be a very perverse individual. And it is also generally understood that a party hardly ever goes the way it is planned or intended. This last, of course, excludes those dismal slave parties, whipped and controlled and dominated, given by ogreish professional hostesses. These are not parties at all, but acts and demonstrations, about as spontaneous as peristalsis and as interesting as its end product.

Probably everyone in Cannery Row had projected his imagination to how the party would be – the shouts of greeting, the congratulations, the noise and good feeling. And it didn't start that way at all. Promptly at eight o'clock Mack and the boys, combed and clean, picked up their jugs and marched down the chicken-walk, over the railroad track, through the lot across the street and up the steps of Western Biological. Everyone was embarrassed. Doc held the door open and Mack made a little speech. 'Being as how it's your birthday, I and the boys thought we would wish you happy birthday and we got twenty-one cats for you for a present.'

He stopped and they stood forlornly on the stairs.

'Come on in,' said Doc. 'Why – I'm – surprised. I didn't even know you knew it was my birthday.'

'All tom-cats,' said Hazel. 'We didn't bring 'em down.'

They sat down formally in the room at the left. There was a long silence. 'Well,' said Doc, 'now you're here, how about a little drink?'

Mack said: 'We brought a little snort,' and he indicated the three jugs Eddie had been accumulating. 'They ain't no beer in it,' said Eddie.

Doc covered his early evening reluctance. 'No,' he said. 'You've got to have a drink with me. It just happens I laid in some whisky.'

They were just seated formally, sipping delicately at the whisky, when Dora and the girls came in. They presented the quilt. Doc laid it over his bed and it was beautiful. And they accepted a little drink. Mr and Mrs Malloy followed with their presents.

'Lots of folks don't know what this stuff's going to be worth,' said Sam Malloy as he brought out the Chalmers 1916 piston and connecting-rod. 'There probably isn't three of these here left in the world.'

And now people began to arrive in droves. Henri came in with a pin cushion three by four feet. He wanted to give a lecture on his new art form, but by this time the formality was broken. Mr and Mrs Gay came in. Lee Chong presented the great string of fire-crackers and the China lily bulbs. Someone ate the lily bulbs by eleven o'clock, but the fire-crackers lasted longer. A group of comparative strangers came in from 'La Ida'. The stiffness was going out of the party quickly. Dora sat in a kind of throne, her orange hair flaming. She held her whisky-glass daintily, with her little finger extended. And she kept an eye on the girls to see that they conducted themselves properly. Doc put dance music on the phonograph and he went to the kitchen and began to fry the steaks.

The first fight was not a bad one. One of the group from 'La Ida' made an immoral proposal to one of Dora's girls. She protested and Mack and the boys, outraged at this breach of propriety, threw him out quickly and without breaking anything. They felt good then, for they knew they were contributing.

Out in the kitchen Doc was frying steaks in three skillets,

and he cut up tomatoes and piled up sliced bread. He felt very good. Mack was personally taking care of the phonograph. He had found an album of Benny Goodman's trios. Dancing had started, indeed the party was beginning to take on depth and vigour. Eddie went into the office and did a tap-dance. Doc had taken a pint with him to the kitchen and he helped himself from the bottle. He was feeling better and better. Everyone was surprised when he served the meat. Nobody was really hungry and they cleaned it up instantly. Now the food set the party into a kind of rich digestive sadness. The whisky was gone and Doc brought out the gallons of wine.

Dora, sitting enthroned, said: 'Doc, play some of that nice music. I get Christ awful sick of that musical-box over home.'

Then Doc played *Ardo* and the *Amor* from an album of Monteverdi. And the guests sat quietly and their eyes were inward. Dora breathed beauty. Two newcomers crept up the stairs and entered quietly. Doc was feeling a golden pleasant sadness. The guests were silent when the music stopped. Doc brought out a book and he read in a clear, deep voice:

> Even now
> If I see in my soul the citron-breasted fair one
> Still gold-tinted, her face like our night stars,
> Drawing unto her; her body beaten about with flame,
> Wounded by the flaring spear of love,
> My first of all by reason of her fresh years,
> Then is my heart buried alive in snow.
>
> Even now
> If my girl with lotus eyes came to me again
> Weary with the dear weight of young love,
> Again I would give her to these starved twins of arms
> And from her mouth drink down the heavy wine,
> As a reeling pirate bee in fluttered ease
> Steals up the honey from the nenuphar.
>
> Even now
> If I saw her lying all wide eyes

And with collyrium the indent of her cheek
Lengthened to the bright ear and her pale side
So suffering the fever of my distance,
Then would my love for her be ropes of flowers, and night
A black-haired lover on the breasts of day.

Even now
My eyes that hurry to see no more are painting, painting
Faces of my lost girl. O golden rings
That tap against cheeks of small magnolia-leaves,
O whitest so soft parchment where
My poor divorcèd lips have written excellent
Stanzas of kisses, and will write no more.

Even now
Death sends me the flickering of powdery lids
Over wild eyes and the pity of her slim body
All broken up with the weariness of joy;
The little red flowers of her breasts to be my comfort
Moving above scarves, and for my sorrow
Wet crimson lips that once I marked as mine.

Even now
They chatter her weakness through the two bazaars
Who was so strong to love me. And small men
That buy and sell for silver being slaves
Crinkles the fat about their eyes; and yet
No Prince of the Cities of the Sea has taken her,
Leading to his grim bed. Little lonely one,
You cling to me as a garment clings; my girl.

Even now
I love long black eyes that caress like silk,
Ever and ever sad and laughing eyes,
Whose lids make such sweet shadow when they close
It seems another beautiful look of hers.
I love a fresh mouth, ah, a scented mouth,
And curving hair, subtle as a smoke,
And light fingers, and laughter of green gems.

Even now
I remember that you made answer very softly,

We being one soul, your hand on my hair,
The burning memory rounding your near lips;
I have seen the priestesses of Rati make love at moon fall
And then in a carpeted hall with a bright gold lamp
Lie down carelessly anywhere to sleep.*

Phyllis Mae was openly weeping when he stopped and
Dora herself dabbed at her eyes. Hazel was so taken by the
sound of the words that he had not listened to their mean-
ing. But a little world sadness had slipped over all of them.
Everyone was remembering a lost love, everyone a call.

Mack said: 'Jesus, that's pretty. Reminds me of a dame
. . .' and he let it pass. They filled the wineglasses and became quiet. The party was slipping away in sweet sadness.
Eddie went out in the office and did a little tap-dance and
came back and sat down again. The party was about to
recline and go to sleep when there was a tramp of feet on
the stairs. A great voice shouted: 'Where's the girls?'

Mack got up almost happily and crossed quickly to the
door. And a smile of joy illuminated the faces of Hughie and
Jones. 'What girls you got in mind?' Mack asked softly.

'Ain't this a whore-house? Cab-driver said they was one
down here.'

'You made a mistake, Mister.' Mack's voice was gay.

'Well, what's them dames in there?'

They joined battle then. They were the crew of a San
Pedro tuna-boat, good, hard, happy, fight-wise men. With
the first rush they burst through to the party. Dora's girls
had each one slipped off a shoe and held it by the toe. As
the fight raged by they would clip a man on the head with
the spike heel. Dora leaped for the kitchen and came roaring
out with a meat grinder. Even Doc was happy. He flailed
about with the Chalmers 1916 piston and connecting-rod.

It was a good fight. Hazel tripped and got kicked in the
face twice before he could get to his feet again. The Franklin

Black Marigolds, translated from the Sanskrit by E. Powys Mathers.

stove went over with a crash. Driven to a corner the newcomers defended themselves with heavy books from the bookcases. But gradually they were driven back. The two front windows were broken out. Suddenly Alfred, who had heard the trouble from across the street, attacked from the rear with his favourite weapon, an indoor ball bat. The fight raged down the steps and into the street and across into the lot. The front door was hanging limply from one hinge again. Doc's shirt was torn off and his slight strong shoulder dripped blood from a scratch. The enemy was driven halfway up the lot when the sirens sounded. Doc's birthday-party had barely time to get inside the laboratory and wedge the broken door closed and turn out the lights before the police car cruised up. The cops didn't find anything. But the party was sitting in the dark giggling happily and drinking wine. The shift changed at the Bear Flag. The fresh contingent raged in full of hell. And then the party really got going. The cops came back, looked in, clicked their tongues and joined it. Mack and the boys used the squad car to go to Jimmy Brucia's for more wine and Jimmy came back with them. You could hear the roar of the party from end to end of Cannery Row. The party had all the best qualities of a riot and a night on the barricades. The crew from the San Pedro tuna-boat crept humbly back and joined the party. They were embraced and admired. A woman five blocks away called the police to complain about the noise and couldn't get anyone. The cops reported their own car stolen and found it later on the beach. Doc sitting cross-legged on the table smiled and tapped his fingers gently on his knee. Mack and Phyllis Mae were doing Indian wrestling on the floor. And the cool bay wind blew in through the broken windows. It was then that someone lighted the twenty-five-foot string of fire-crackers.

CHAPTER XXXI

A WELL-GROWN gopher took up residence in a thicket of mallow weeds in the vacant lot on Cannery Row. It was a perfect place. The deep green luscious mallows towered up crisp and rich, and as they matured their little cheeses hung down provocatively. The earth was perfect for a gopher-hole too, black and soft and yet with a little clay in it so that it didn't crumble and the tunnels didn't cave in. The gopher was fat and sleek and he had always plenty of food in his cheek pouches. His little ears were clean and well set and his eyes were as black as old-fashioned pin-heads and just about the same size. His digging hands were strong and the fur on his back was glossy brown and the fawn-coloured fur on his chest was incredibly soft and rich. He had long curving yellow teeth and a little short tail. Altogether he was a beautiful gopher and in the prime of his life.

He came to the place over-land and found it good and he began his burrow on a little eminence where he could look out among the mallow weeds and see the trucks go by on Cannery Row. He could watch the feet of Mack and the boys as they crossed the lot to the Palace Flophouse. As he dug down into the coal-black earth he found it even more perfect, for there were great rocks under the soil. When he made his great chamber for the storing of food it was under a rock so that it could never cave in, no matter how hard it rained. It was a place where he could settle down and raise any number of families and the burrow could increase in all directions.

It was beautiful in the early morning when he first poked

his head out of the burrow. The mallows filtered green light down on him and the first rays of the rising sun shone into his hole and warmed it so that he lay there content and very comfortable.

When he had dug his great chamber and his four emergency exits and his waterproof deluge room, the gopher began to store food. He cut down only the perfect mallow stems and trimmed them to the exact length he needed and he took them down the hole and stacked them neatly in his great chamber, and arranged them so they wouldn't ferment or get sour. He had found the perfect place to live. There were no gardens about, so no one would think of setting a trap for him. Cats there were, many of them, but they were so bloated with fish-heads and guts from the canneries that they had long ago given up hunting. The soil was sandy enough, so that water never stood about or filled a hole for long. The gopher worked and worked until he had his great chamber crammed with food. Then he made little side chambers for the babies who would inhabit them. In a few years there might be thousands of his progeny spreading out from this original hearthstone.

But as time went on the gopher began to be a little impatient, for no female appeared. He sat in the entrance of his hole in the morning and made penetrating squeaks that are inaudible to the human ear but can be heard deep in the earth by other gophers. And still no female appeared. Finally in a sweat of impatience he went up across the track until he found another gopher-hole. He squeaked provocatively in the entrance. He heard a rustling and smelled female, and then out of the hole came an old battle-torn bull gopher who mauled and bit him so badly that he crept home and lay in his great chamber for three days recovering and he lost two toes from one front paw from that fight.

Again he waited and squeaked beside his beautiful burrow in the beautiful place, but no female ever came, and after a while he had to move away. He had to move two blocks up the hill to a dahlia garden where they put out traps every night.

CHAPTER XXXII

Doc awakened very slowly and clumsily like a fat man getting out of a swimming-pool. His mind broke the surface and fell back several times. There was red lipstick on his beard. He opened one eye, saw the brilliant colours of the quilt, and closed his eye quickly. But after a while he looked again. His eye went past the quilt to the floor, to the broken plate in the corner, to the glasses standing on the table turned over on the floor, to the spilled wine and the books like heavy fallen butterflies. There were little bits of curled red paper all over the place and the sharp smell of fire-crackers. He could see through the kitchen door to the steak plates stacked high and the skillets deep in grease. Hundreds of cigarette-butts were stamped out on the floor. And under the fire-cracker smell was a fine combination of wine and whisky and perfume. His eye stopped for a moment on a little pile of hairpins in the middle of the floor.

He rolled over slowly and supporting himself on one elbow he looked out the broken window. Cannery Row was quiet and sunny. The boiler door was open. The door of the Palace Flophouse was closed. A man slept peacefully among the weeds in the vacant lot. The Bear Flag was shut up tight.

Doc got up and went into the kitchen and lighted the gas water-heater on his way to the toilet. Then he came back and sat on the edge of his bed and worked his toes together while he surveyed the wreckage. From up the hill he could hear the church bells ringing. When the gas heater began rumbling he went back to the bathroom and took a shower and he put on blue jeans and a flannel shirt. Lee Chong was closed, but he saw who was at the door and opened it. He went to the refrigerator and brought out a quart of beer without being asked. Doc paid him.

'Good time?' Lee asked. His brown eyes were a little inflamed in their pouches.

'Good time!' said Doc, and he went back to the laboratory with his cold beer. He made a peanut-butter sandwich to eat with his beer. It was very quiet in the street. No one went by at all. Doc heard music in his head – violas and 'cellos, he thought. And they played cool, soft, soothing music with nothing much to distinguish it. He ate his sandwich and sipped his beer and listened to the music. When he had finished his beer, Doc went into the kitchen, and cleared the dirty dishes out of the sink. He ran hot water in it and poured soap chips under the running water so that the foam stood high and white. Then he moved about collecting all the glasses that weren't broken. He put them in the soapy hot water. The steak-plates were piled high on the stove with their brown juice and their white grease sticking them together. Doc cleared a place on the table for the clean glasses as he washed them. Then he unlocked the door of the back room and brought out one of his albums of Gregorian music and he put a Paternoster and Agnus Dei on the turntable and started it going. The angelic, disembodied voices filled the laboratory. They were incredibly pure and sweet. Doc worked carefully washing the glasses so that they would not clash together and spoil the music. The boys' voices carried the melody up and down, simply but with the richness that is in no other singing. When the record had finished, Doc wiped his hands and turned it off. He saw a book lying half under his bed and picked it up and he sat down on the bed. For a moment he read to himself, but then his lips began to move and in a moment he read aloud – slowly, pausing at the end of each line.

Even now
I mind the coming and talking of wise men from towers
Where they had thought away their youth. And I, listening,
Found not the salt of the whispers of my girl,
Murmur of confused colours, as we lay near sleep;
Little wise words and little witty words,
Wanton as water, honied with eagerness.

In the sink the high white foam cooled and ticked as the bubbles burst. Under the piers it was very high tide and the waves splashed on rocks they had not reached in a long time.

Even now
I mind that I loved cypress and roses, clear,
The great blue mountains and the small grey hills,
The sounding of the sea. Upon a day
I saw strange eyes and hands like butterflies;
For me at morning larks flew from the thyme
And children came to bathe in little streams.

Doc closed the book. He could hear the waves beat under the piles and he could hear the scampering of white rats against the wire. He went into the kitchen and felt the cooling water in the sink. He ran hot water into it. He spoke aloud to the sink and the white rats, and to himself:

Even now
I know that I have savoured the hot taste of life
Lifting green cups and gold at the great feast.
Just for a small and a forgotten time
I have had full in my eyes from off my girl
The whitest pouring of eternal light . . .

He wiped his eyes with the back of his hand. And the white rats scampered and scrambled in their cages. And behind the glass the rattlesnakes lay still and stared into space with their dusty, frowning eyes.

John Steinbeck
Burning Bright £1.50

A powerful human drama of two men – one sterile of body, one sterile
of mind – and a woman capable of any lie or cheat or violence for her
husband's happiness.

East of Eden £2.95

'This is his finest work. There is no more impressive writer on either
side of the Atlantic' TIME AND TIDE

Sweet Thursday £1.95

'His most likeable and lively book for several years' PUNCH

The Grapes of Wrath £2.50

'This is a terrible and indignant book; yet it is not without passages of
lyrical beauty, and the ultimate impression is that of the dignity of the
human spirit under the stress of the most desperate conditions'
GUARDIAN

The Moon is Down £1.50

A great novel of courage, defiance and human dignity under stress
tells with stunning power and rich humanity how invasion came to a
small Norwegian town – and how the inhabitants met their
conquerors.

John Steinbeck
The Pearl £1.25

Perfect as the moon, the great pearl turned Kino the fisherman into
every man's enemy. The dreams he conjured from its shining surface
were to bring sorrow and death.

The Winter of our Discontent £2.50

'Not since *East of Eden* has Steinbeck engated a theme of such broad
social significance. Not since *The Grapes of Wrath* has he found a
subject closer to his heart' NEW YORK TIMES BOOK REVIEW

Also available

The Log from the Sea of Cortez £2.50
The Short Reign of Pippin IV £1.95

Classes

☐	**Emma**		£1.50p
☐	**Mansfield Park**		£1.25p
☐	**Northanger Abbey**		95p
☐	**Persuasion**	Jane Austen	£1.25p
☐	**Pride and Prejudice**		£1.25p
☐	**Sense and Sensibility**		£1.25p
☐	**The Old Wives' Tale**	Arnold Bennett	£1.95p
☐	**Lorna Doone**	R. D. Blackmore	£1.95p
☐	**Jane Eyre**	Charlotte Brontë	£1.50p
☐	**Villette**		£1.75p
☐	**Wuthering Heights**	Emily Brontë	£1.25p
☐	**The Woman in White**	Wilkie Collins	£1.95p
☐	**The Moonstone**		£1.50p
☐	**Nostromo**	Joseph Conrad	£1.25p
☐	**The Divine Comedy**	Dante trans. C. H. Sisson	£3.50p
☐	**David Copperfield**		£1.95p
☐	**Great Expectations**	Charles Dickens	£1.50p
☐	**Nicholas Nickleby**		£1.95p
☐	**Oliver Twist**		£1.50p
☐	**Crime and Punishment**	Fyodor Dostoevsky	£1.50p
☐	**Middlemarch**	George Eliot	£1.95p
☐	**The Mill on the Floss**		£1.95p
☐	**Far From the Madding Crowd**		£1.50p
☐	**The Mayor of Casterbridge**		£1.25p
☐	**The Return of the Native**	Thomas Hardy	£1.50p
☐	**Tess of the D'Urbervilles**		£1.75p
☐	**The Trumpet-Major**		£1.50p
☐	**The Woodlanders**		£1.50p
☐	**Perelandra**	C. S. Lewis	£1.95p
☐	**That Hideous Strength**		£2.50p
☐	**The Republic**	Plato trans. G. M. A. Grube	£2.95p
☐	**Vanity Fair**	William Thackeray	£1.95p
☐	**Anna Karenina**	Leo Tolstoy	£3.95p
☐	**War and Peace**		£4.95p
☐	**Barchester Towers**	Anthony Trollope	£1.95p
☐	**The History of Mr Polly**	H. G. Wells	£1.95p
☐	**Tono Bungay**		£1.95p

Poetry and drama

☐	**Church Poems**	John Betjeman	£1.95p
☐	**The Prophet**	Kahlil Gibran	£1.95p
☐	**W. B. Yeats Selected Plays**	⎱ edited by	£2.95p
☐	**W. B. Yeats Selected Poetry**	⎰ Norman Jeffares	£1.95p
☐	**The New Golden Treasury** **of English Verse**	ed. E. G. Leeson	£2.50p
☐	**For Services Rendered**	W. Somerset Maugham	£1.50p
☐	**Three Plays**	Sean O'Casey	£2.50p

Literature guides

☐	**An Introduction to Shakespeare** **and his Contemporaries**	Marguerite Alexander	£2.95p
☐	**An Introduction to Fifty** **Modern British Plays**	Benedict Nightingale	£2.95p
☐	**An Introduction to Fifty** **Modern European Poets**	John Pilling	£2.95p
☐	**An Introduction to Fifty** **Modern British Poets**	Michael Schmidt	£1.95p
☐	**An Introduction to Fifty** **European Novels**	Martin Seymour-Smith	£1.95p

All these books are available at your local bookshop or newsagent, or can be ordered direct from the publisher. Indicate the number of copies required and fill in the form below 12

....

Name_____
(Block letters please)

Address_____

_____

Send to CS Department, Pan Books Ltd, PO Box 40, Basingstoke, Hants
Please enclose remittance to the value of the cover price plus:
35p for the first book plus 15p per copy for each additional book ordered
to a maximum charge of £1.25 to cover postage and packing
Applicable only in the UK

While every effort is made to keep prices low, it is sometimes
necessary to increase prices at short notice. Pan Books reserve
the right to show on covers and charge new retail prices which
may differ from those advertised in the text or elsewhere